SHIPMENT ONE

Tex Times Ten by Tina Leonard
Runaway Cowboy by Judy Christenberry
Crazy for Lovin' You by Teresa Southwick
The Rancher Next Door by Cathy Gillen Thacker
Intimate Secrets by B.J. Daniels
Operation: Texas by Roxanne Rustand

SHIPMENT TWO

Navarro or Not by Tina Leonard
Trust a Cowboy by Judy Christenberry
Taming a Dark Horse by Stella Bagwell
The Rancher's Family Thanksgiving by Cathy Gillen Thacker
The Valentine Two-Step by RaeAnne Thayne
The Cowboy and the Bride by Marin Thomas

SHIPMENT THREE

Catching Calhoun by Tina Leonard
The Christmas Cowboy by Judy Christenberry
The Come-Back Cowboy by Jodi O'Donnell
The Rancher's Christmas Baby by Cathy Gillen Thacker
Baby Love by Victoria Pade
The Best Catch in Texas by Stella Bagwell
This Kiss by Teresa Southwick

SHIPMENT FOUR

Archer's Angels by Tina Leonard
More to Texas than Cowboys by Roz Denny Fox
The Rancher's Promise by Jodi O'Donnell
The Gentleman Rancher by Cathy Gillen Thacker
Cowboy's Baby by Victoria Pade
Having the Cowboy's Baby by Stella Bagwell

SHIPMENT FIVE

Belonging to Bandera by Tina Leonard
Court Me, Cowboy by Barbara White Daille
His Best Friend's Bride by Jodi O'Donnell
The Cowboy's Return by Linda Warren
Baby Be Mine by Victoria Pade
The Cattle Baron by Margaret Way

SHIPMENT SIX

Crockett's Seduction by Tina Leonard
Coming Home to the Cattleman by Judy Christenberry
Almost Perfect by Judy Duarte
Cowboy Dad by Cathy McDavid
Real Cowboys by Roz Denny Fox
The Rancher Wore Suits by Rita Herron
Falling for the Texas Tycoon by Karen Rose Smith

SHIPMENT SEVEN

Last's Temptation by Tina Leonard
Daddy by Choice by Marin Thomas
The Cowboy, the Baby and the Bride-to-Be by Cara Colter
Luke's Proposal by Lois Faye Dyer
The Truth About Cowboys by Margot Early
The Other Side of Paradise by Laurie Paige

SHIPMENT EIGHT

Mason's Marriage by Tina Leonard
Bride at Briar's Ridge by Margaret Way
Texas Bluff by Linda Warren
Cupid and the Cowboy by Carol Finch
The Horseman's Son by Delores Fossen
Cattleman's Bride-to-Be by Lois Faye Dyer

The rugged, masculine and independent men of America's West know the value of hard work, honor and family. They may be ranchers, tycoons or the guy next door, but they're all cowboys at heart. Don't miss any of the books in this collection!

TRUST A COWBOY

JUDY CHRISTENBERRY

HARLEQUIN® COWBOY AT HEART

Recycling programs for this product may not exist in your area.

ISBN-13: 978-0-373-82609-4

TRUST A COWBOY

This edition published by arrangement with Harlequin Books S.A.

For questions and comments about the quality of this book, please contact us at CustomerService@Harlequin.com.

Printed in U.S.A.

JUDY CHRISTENBERRY

has written more than eighty-five books for Harlequin Romance, Harlequin American Romance and Harlequin Intrigue. She spends her spare time reading and watching her favorite sports teams. Judy lives in Texas.

Chapter One

Pete Ledbetter watched his grandfather lift his glass of champagne to the employees of the Lazy L Ranch, near Steamboat Springs, Colorado. They were celebrating the end of their first season as both a working cattle operation and a dude ranch.

It had been a long summer, and now Pete looked forward to eight weeks of vacation, except for taking care of the cattle, of course. At least he'd have his brother's help with that.

But what was he going to do about Mary Jo?

He'd apologized, of course, but didn't think she'd accepted it. What worried him was that he believed she was leaving the ranch at the end of the month.

He couldn't blame her. All the blame

rested on him. Last summer, he'd had the greatest night of his life with Mary Jo, but two days later he'd made a colossal mistake by sleeping with a guest. He'd let himself be taken in by the city girl's sweet talkin' flattery and come-hither smile. He hadn't thought about the ramifications of his action. But Mary Jo had. And quickly.

She'd given notice.

As the ranch chef, she played a big role in keeping their guests happy. Not only did Pete need to make amends for himself, he had to for the sake of the dude ranch, as well.

"Aren't you glad the first season is over?" Cliff Ledbetter asked him, a big grin on his face.

"Sure, Granddad." Pete mustered up a smile. He'd been against the idea of turning the Lazy L into a dude ranch after his parents' death, but Granddad and Jessie, his sister, had decided to go ahead. Their plan had worked out because Granddad had brought in Jim Bradford as manager.

Jim had gotten the job done, in spite of Pete's lack of cooperation, and he'd married Jessica to boot. All Pete had gotten last summer was a broken leg, thanks to his own stupidity.

"Granddad, what are Mary Jo's plans?"

Cliff stared at him. "She said she'd cook for the month of October, while Jessie and Jim are on their honeymoon, didn't she?"

"Yeah, I know, but what about…afterward?"

"We haven't asked her to sign a contract for the winter season yet. I can take care of that in a couple of weeks."

Pete didn't want to say too much. Not today. And not when Mary Jo could overhear on her trips in and out of the kitchen.

She had to be tired, he thought. After all, she'd prepared breakfast for everyone that morning, and then put together their lunch celebration.

Without another thought, he got to his feet, picked up one of the plastic tubs and started gathering up dirty dishes. When it was full he followed Mary Jo into the kitchen.

"You don't need to do that, Pete. It's

my job." She kept her face averted as she worked.

"You've done more than your share, Mary Jo. It doesn't hurt me to help a little."

Edith, Mary Jo's second-in-command, came in with another tub of dirty dishes. "Because of Pete, there wasn't much left for me to clean up."

"That was nice of him, wasn't it?" Mary Jo said, still not looking at him.

Pete wasn't fooled by her praise. He knew he needed to talk to her again, but this wasn't the time. Stoically, he began to rinse plates and glasses, stacking them in the dishwasher.

Half an hour later, when he finally left the kitchen, he ran into his brother, who was three years younger than him.

"Hey, Pete, how'd you get stuck doing the dishes today?" Hank asked.

"Mary Jo shouldn't have to do all that alone. Wouldn't kill you to help out this month, either."

Hank gave him a strange look. "Are you feeling all right?"

He shook his head. "What do you have planned for this afternoon?"

"Putting my feet up," his brother exclaimed with a grin.

"Want to go for a ride?"

He nodded. "Sure. Why not?"

"Good. I'm going to ask Mary Jo to join us."

"Maybe you'd prefer for me to stay home?"

"No! She won't go with just me, but I think she'd enjoy a ride today."

"Okay, bro. I'll come along. I'll go saddle the horses while you persuade her."

Pete went back to the kitchen, but it was empty. He checked the main rooms, then finally went to the staff area and knocked on Mary Jo's door.

She opened it, but when she saw him, she closed it to a mere slit. "What do you want, Pete?"

"Hank and I are going for a ride, now that lunch is over. Would you like to come?"

"Hank is going, too?" she asked.

"Yeah. He's out saddling the horses."

"You're sure I can come?"

"I'm sure."

"All right. I have to change. Then I'll be down there."

"Great." He immediately left for the barn, not wanting to hang around and scare her off. During the season, they hadn't had time to work out their problems. But Pete needed to do so now—he wanted her to stay.

Time was running out.

MARY JO OPENED the door to her room, looking around for Pete, fearing he might be waiting for her. It wasn't that she didn't like him. The problem was she liked him too much.

Still, she didn't intend to have anything to do with him. Ever again.

But she did want to ride, and since Hank would be joining them she wouldn't have to be alone with Pete. Because it could get chilly in the Rockies even in early October, she tied a jacket around her waist and set off for the barn.

Once there, she cautiously looked around for Hank. With relief, she saw him talking with his brother as they saddled up Biscuit, her favorite mount.

"You ready to ride, Mary Jo?" Hank asked when they were done.

"Yes, if you are." She held her breath, realizing that he might decline at the last minute. She didn't exhale until he climbed into the saddle.

"Let's go."

She and Pete mounted, and Mary Jo finally relaxed. Over the summer she'd discovered a real affinity for horseback riding. She'd been on horses before she came to the Lazy L, but never on a regular basis. Once her schedule had gotten worked out so she had steady days off, she'd ridden twice every week.

"Let's take the trail down by the stream," Pete suggested. "I want to see how deep it's running."

The aspen leaves were golden now and the wind blew through them, making them quiver. Mary Jo loved this time of the year—the colors, the smells, the briskness in the air. She breathed deeply, absorbing every detail, until Pete rode up beside her.

"We came through the first season of the dude ranch very well, I think. We learned a lot, too. Don't you agree, Mary Jo?"

"Yes, of course."

"I want you to know I'm not going to fight Jim and Jessie anymore."

Riding alongside him, she nodded. "They've certainly proved themselves this summer."

"And Hank's agreed to follow their suggestions, too. He's going to cull a few horses from guest status."

"He is? Which horses?"

"You won't believe it, but Biscuit's one. She's better off with one of us riding her." His eyes raked Mary Jo from head to toe. "See? You don't have a problem with her at all."

Something about the way Pete looked at her made her cheeks flame. Quickly, she looked down at her mount. "N-no, of course not. She's a perfect lady."

His response did nothing to cool her down. In a suddenly husky voice he said, "That's because she's got a perfect lady riding her."

PETE WATCHED MARY JO closely. She kept her distance from him, and he couldn't blame her. She'd trusted him once, and then he'd betrayed her. He hadn't realized it at the time, until Jim had explained it to him. Pete had been careless with her heart and he regretted it.

Didn't matter. No matter how apologetic he was, she wasn't going to trust him. But he hoped they could at least become friends again.

"Hey, Mary Jo, do you want to herd cattle with us this month?" he asked suddenly.

She swung around, and the expression on her face was one of terror. "No! I'll cook for you, but I can't herd cattle."

He laughed. "I was just teasing. We'll settle for your excellent cooking. But you've really become a good rider."

"Thank you."

"What are your plans after this month? Are you going to take a trip?" Pete asked.

"I—I haven't decided." Her cheeks flared red again.

Despite her answer, he was worried about the future. Hank had ridden a little ahead, and this was the best chance Pete was going to have to talk to her. He cleared his throat and launched right into his prepared speech. “Mary Jo, I know I made a mistake when I didn’t take things seriously between us, but I’ve apologized before and I’ll apologize again today. Please, can’t you forgive me?”

Her chin came up and she stared straight ahead. “I forgive you, Pete. But I haven’t forgotten.”

With a silent groan, he closed his eyes. “Okay, I understand you haven’t forgotten. But can’t we at least be friends?”

“What difference does it make?”

“I don’t want you to go!” Careful not to reveal too much, he corrected, “I mean *we* don’t want you to leave the ranch.”

“I’ll be here until November.”

“Come on, Mary Jo. Think of us. We need your good cooking.”

“You can easily find another chef, Pete. I’m sure that won’t be a problem.”

“We won’t be able to find one like—”

“Hey, are you two coming?” Hank called over his shoulder.

Pete stifled a curse. His brother *would* have to choose that moment to interrupt. Mary Jo clucked to Biscuit to catch up with Hank, and Pete knew the moment was over.

But he wouldn't give up. He had to make her stay. He might be offering friendship, but what he really wanted was for her to love him again.

THEY HAD CROSSED the icy stream and gone into the next pasture, closer to the mountains. When they topped a hill, Hank halted.

"What's wrong?" Pete asked.

"I don't like the look of the sky. Did you check the weather before you came out?"

"No, it didn't occur to me. Why?"

"I think we're going to get a storm."

Pete scanned the sky. It was no longer blue, and a layer of dark clouds was moving in. "We'd better start back," he agreed, nodding abruptly.

"What kind of storm?" Mary Jo asked.

"I believe we're going to get our first snowstorm. At least up here. It may just be rain close to the house."

"Oh. I didn't bring my slicker." She had put her jacket on awhile ago, as soon as they'd neared the mountains.

"It's my fault," Hank mumbled. "I should've tied some rain gear on the saddles."

"It's all right, Hank," Pete said. "We'll turn back, and if we move quickly, we might beat the weather."

They headed toward home, riding at a lope to try and reach the barn before the storm broke. When it did, they were still quite a ways out. And instead of occasional flakes, almost at once the snow began falling fast and furiously.

Hank pulled up. "We can't ride in this. I know a place near here where we can take cover until the storm ends."

He turned in a southerly direction, and the other two followed him. When he rode under an outcropping of rock he halted his horse and dismounted. "This will be better than trying to ride through the snow."

"But wouldn't it be better to press on to the barn?" Mary Jo asked.

"No. We'll wait until the storm stops. I'll build a fire and we'll be okay."

Pete was beside her before she realized it. "Come on, Mary Jo, let me help you down. Hank and I will gather firewood while we can still see."

"Let me help," she answered.

"You're not going out, Mary Jo. Hank and I will do it. You stay here and keep the horses from wandering off."

He could tell she wanted to protest, but she remained silent.

He and Hank moved out into the storm and began looking for wood. It wasn't easy, with snow swirling in their faces and already covering the ground. When both he and Hank had an armful, they returned to the shelter.

"You stay here and get the fire started, Hank. I'll look for more wood," Pete offered.

"Okay, but don't go too far," his brother warned.

Mary Jo watched Pete go back out into the storm, immediately losing sight of him. She might be angry with him, but she didn't want him hurt, or lost in a snowstorm. She remembered when she'd first met him. He was tall and lean and darkly handsome, and something about him had tugged on her heart.

When he'd flirted with her, she'd responded. When he kissed her, she'd wanted more. So much more that she went to bed with him.

Then, two days later, he'd slept with one of the guests.

It seemed he didn't think she'd mind. Or that she had any right to mind. But she did. She'd told him they were through. He'd been so angry, he'd barked ridiculous orders at her, as if she were a ranch hand. She'd immediately done the opposite of what he'd ordered her to do, and he'd been so upset, he'd charged across the room, then promptly fallen and broken his leg. Now he claimed he'd learned his lesson. Still, she doubted that. Men like Pete seldom changed.

So why was she so worried about him now?

"He'll be all right," Hank said softly, catching her eye.

"Oh! Oh, yes, but…but what if he can't find his way back?"

"He will. Just be patient."

She nodded. After all, what could she say?

Hank had gotten a small fire going and was adding larger pieces of wood to it. She felt the heat and suddenly realized how cold she was. That made her much more anxious for Pete to return.

When a snow-covered monster came out of the storm, she almost didn't recognize Pete at all. She ran to him, brushing the snow from his shoulders. "Are you all right?"

"Yeah," he growled. "But visibility is almost down to nothing. I don't think we could've made it back."

"I know." Hank got up and moved to his horse. "My sleeping bag is tied to my saddle. The three of us can share it, and sit comfortably by the fire."

"You don't have any food tied to your saddle, too, do you?" Pete asked.

"Some beef jerky is all. It doesn't compare to Mary Jo's cooking, I'm afraid," he said with a grin. "But it's better than nothing."

Mary Jo chewed her bottom lip. Sharing a sleeping bag with Pete in any circumstance didn't thrill her. But sitting on the bare rock floor wouldn't be comfortable, either. Hank spread out the sleeping bag near the stone slab behind the fire, but she didn't move, unsure what to do.

"Come on, Mary Jo. I promise not to bite." Pete must have realized he'd said the wrong thing because he quickly added, "I mean, I won't crowd you."

Hank added his encouragement. "Yeah, Mary Jo, sit in the middle. I can't see myself cuddling up next to Pete to keep warm."

"I—I'm not cold," she protested, trying not to shiver.

"Then you definitely need to be in the middle. You can keep both of us warm," Pete told her.

With reluctance, she did as the men asked. When she was settled on the sleeping bag, she held out her hands to the warmth of the flames. "How long do you think the wood will last?"

"Long enough," Hank answered. "I'm not building up the fire, because this is all the heat we need. We'll use the wood slowly."

"Okay," she said.

Pete leaned back against the stone wall, trying to relax. He wasn't touching Mary Jo, but he was tempted.

When Hank asked if either of them wanted some beef jerky, Pete shook his head. "Better save it for evening."

"Do you think we'll be here that long?"

He could hear the quiver in Mary Jo's voice and he longed to wrap his arm around her. But he knew she wouldn't welcome his touch.

"We don't know, Mary Jo," he said. "But when the storm stops, we'll be able to find our way to the barn. So don't worry."

"No…I won't worry."

He caught her looking at him out of the corner of her eye. "Are you warm enough?"

"Yes." After a minute, she added, "I'm still a little cold, but it's not as bad."

"You were very brave during our ride." Pete risked a smile, hoping she wouldn't withdraw.

She didn't say anything, but released a shuddering breath.

He leaned in a little. "We're going to get you home safely, honey, I promise."

"I know." She sounded a little more confident. Then she squared her shoulders. "But you shouldn't call me that."

He had to think back to remember what he'd said. "I hoped we'd still be friends, if nothing else."

Hank was messing with the fire, pretending not to listen.

After a moment, Mary Jo said, "I—I guess we can be."

Pete breathed a sigh of relief. It was a start.

FIVE HOURS LATER, Mary Jo was asleep against Pete's shoulder. Awake, she never would have relaxed that much, but in her sleep, she'd slid closer and snuggled against him.

He enjoyed the feel of her, more than he wanted to. He couldn't help it. It brought back memories of early in the summer, when they'd been a couple. Before he'd blown his chance with her.

He tore his eyes from Mary Jo and looked out of their shelter. "Hank, has the weather eased up?"

"Maybe. The snow seems to have lessened."

"Can we make it to the barn?"

"I think so. But we'll be cold."

"Can we wrap your sleeping bag around Mary Jo to keep her warm?"

"Yeah, that's a good idea."

"Okay. Let's mount up."

Pete leaned his head down and whispered. "Wake up, honey. It's time to go home."

Mary Jo opened her eyes. When she saw how close he was, she immediately shoved him away. Pete missed more than her warmth.

"The snow has let up. We're ready to ride back to the barn."

"Oh! Oh, of course. So we need to get going?"

"Yeah, but we want you to keep warm in the sleeping bag. Climb on Biscuit and I'll wrap you in it."

"What about you and Hank?"

"We'll be all right." Pete stood up and offered her a hand. Pulling her to her feet, he led her to Biscuit. She mounted, and Pete quickly wrapped the sleeping bag around her.

"You'll need to hold it in place, Mary Jo. Your horse will follow Hank's. I'll be right behind you."

Pete checked to be sure Hank had put out the fire, then he swung into the saddle. His brother led the way out into the eerie night, through almost a foot of white snow. The three horses plowed through it doggedly, as if eager to reach home.

After about thirty minutes, Mary Jo lost hold of the sleeping bag. Pete rode up to help her regain her grip. "You need to hold on, Mary Jo. We'll be back at the barn soon. Then we'll get you in the house where it's warm."

"Sounds good," she said.

But for Pete, the thought of going home to a warm house suddenly didn't have as much appeal as their shelter in the snow. At least there he could hold Mary Jo.

Chapter Two

By the time they reached the barn, the horses were dragging, as fatigued as Mary Jo. She suspected the men felt the same way, but they weren't about to show it.

Pete swung down from his horse and helped her dismount. "Keep the sleeping bag around you until we reach the house."

"I will. Should I help unsaddle Biscuit?"

"Nope, we'll manage." Pete started to move away from her, then said, "Why don't you sit on the bench? We won't be long."

He obviously thought she couldn't remember the way to the house, though she'd lived there since last March. But she settled down, wrapped in the sleeping bag. With her head against the stall behind her, she shut her eyes and relaxed.

"Come on, Mary Jo. Time to go to the house."

She looked up to see Pete's face, and realized she must have dozed off. "I can walk by myself," she said, when he reached for her.

"Okay. I was just offering support. There's a strong wind blowing."

"You ready?" Hank asked, coming up to them.

"Yeah. Are you, Mary Jo?"

"Yes, I'm ready."

They moved out of the barn, leaning into the cold wind. She couldn't help shuddering. Pete's arm came around her and she didn't shrug it off.

Hank pulled out a key, unlocked the back door and swung it open. Pete rushed her inside. "Go to your room and take a hot shower. By the time you get out, we'll have leftovers heated up."

"No. I was warmer than either of you because you gave me the sleeping bag. I'll heat up some supper while both of you take a hot shower."

"Mary Jo, we're used to the cold. You aren't. Just—"

"No, Pete, I won't leave either of you to do my job. You've got about fifteen minutes."

Pete turned to Hank. "You heard the lady. Last one back has to do the dishes!"

Both men disappeared into their rooms.

Mary Jo went into the kitchen and washed her hands before taking out leftovers and warming them. She set three places at the table in the kitchen, grateful for the informality after a season of serving guests.

Cliff and Leslie had their own place near the big house now, and Leslie said she was looking forward to cooking for her and her new husband. Mary Jo thought that was sweet. And it relieved her of cooking for two more people.

She was putting dishes on the table when Hank rushed in. "I guess I won, Mary Jo. That leaves Pete to do the cleanup."

Pete hurried in just then, coming to an abrupt halt when he saw his brother. "Damn! I thought I was ahead of you."

"Nope, you lose."

"Take your seats, gentlemen," Mary Jo said.

They all sat down and began their meal. It was nine-thirty, and all three were hungry. They ate in silence, until Mary Jo said, "I want to thank both of you for taking care of me this afternoon. I didn't mean to be such a burden."

"You weren't a burden, Mary Jo," Hank declared.

"You were a good sport," Pete added. "We weren't prepared for a snowstorm, but you handled it well."

"With your help—and the sleeping bag," she added, grinning at them.

Both men smiled at her.

"Well, as your reward, I'll go get you some dessert." She got up to cut pieces of cake.

Pete cleared the table while she was doing so, and Hank sat back, obviously enjoying the sight of his brother working.

"Quit grinning, Hank. Your turn will come," Pete warned.

"Not as long as I'm faster than you."

Pete growled, "I'm not worried about doing the dishes. There's only three of us. But I think we should take turns doing cleanup from now on if Mary Jo is going to cook for us."

"That's not necessary!" she exclaimed.

But Hank was nodding in agreement. "You're right, Pete. We'll do that."

"It's okay, Mary Jo. It's not going to kill us to help out a little."

"But that's what you're paying me for. It makes no sense to do that and then handle the job yourselves."

"Mary Jo, you're doing us a favor. If Hank and I were left to ourselves in the kitchen, we'd starve to death."

"That's true," his brother agreed.

"Well, I'll try out some new recipes and you can give me feedback for…for next year," she murmured.

"I think that's a good plan, though I don't think you could do better than you did last season."

"Thank you, Pete. I—I think for the winter, we'll need some different dishes, some heartier meals."

"Will it be difficult to pack lunches for the skiers each day?"

"Not really. We can start on them as soon as we put out the breakfast buffet. It will make for more work in the morning, and in the afternoon, also. You and Hank will have it easier during the winter months, though, won't you?"

"Yeah, once we bring the cattle down to the lower pastures, they won't require a lot of work. But we should've gotten them rounded up before the first snow."

"Will they be all right tonight?"

"I hope so. The storm wasn't as bad as where we were. We'll start bringing them in tomorrow morning."

"Do you want a packed lunch? I can make you one while you eat breakfast, if you want. It'll be good practice for me, for the winter tourist season."

"That would be great, Mary Jo, if you don't mind." Pete kept an eye on her, waiting for her answer. If she was practicing for the winter session, she might be intending to stay.

"Okay. I'll plan on making two trail lunches tomorrow."

"But—" Hank began.

"That will be great," Pete said as he kicked his brother under the table.

Hank glared at him, but didn't say anything more.

Both men finished their cake, and then Pete began rinsing plates and putting them in the dishwasher. Cleanup only took about ten minutes. Mary Jo swept the floor while Pete was doing the dishes. When he turned away from the sink, he found she had finished also.

"Nice job, Mary Jo."

"Same to you, Pete."

Hank had left the room, and Pete was reluctant to say anything to her now, not after her comment about the winter season. Dare he hope she planned to stay? "I think I'll go on to bed, since I'll be getting up early in the morning."

"Well, thanks for your help, Pete."

"Are you coming to bed, too?" he asked, then wished he could have gobbled the words up, especially when Mary Jo looked at him with wide, dark eyes. "I—I mean are you *going* to bed?"

She merely nodded, saying nothing.

Pete didn't wait for her. He hightailed it out of the kitchen before he could say something wrong again.

THE NEXT MORNING, when Mary Jo presented them with their packed lunches, both men thanked her. But when they walked to the barn in their cold-weather gear, Hank wanted to know what they were going to do with them.

"We can't eat them in front of the men," he said, "unless Cookie is doing the same for them. Maybe we can suggest it to him?"

"We can try."

When they got to the barn, they asked the men if the cook had provided them with some lunch. They all said no.

"Maybe I'd better talk to him," Pete said. He walked to the bunkhouse and went inside. A few minutes later, he came back and said, "Cookie said he'd have packed lunches for you in fifteen minutes. I think we'll all feel better with some food in us when we're dragging in here tonight."

The cowboys were willing to wait. Pete made sure they all had gloves and chaps in the meantime, and when they went back for their lunches, Hank moved over to him.

"What did you have to promise him?"

"A bonus," Pete said under his breath. "But it's worth it if Mary Jo stays." When he saw the amused look on his brother's face, he added, "Her cooking won over a lot of our guests from the start. That's an advantage we don't want to lose." He wasn't about to tell Hank the real reason he didn't want Mary Jo to go.

SHOULD SHE STAY?

The question echoed in Mary Jo's mind all day after the men had ridden out.

She'd admit that her ride yesterday with Pete and Hank had been a breakthrough for her. After all, she hadn't spent much time with Pete since their fight that summer. But she wasn't quite ready to commit to the winter season

Truthfully, she liked this job. And the

Ledbetters liked her. Even Edith had stepped up and taken on the cooking on Wednesdays and Sundays, giving Mary Jo a chance to relax and come up with new dishes for the guests. Not only did she receive a lot of praise from them, she got to work with Jessica, her old college roommate and best friend. This was Mary Jo's dream job and she'd thought she'd never grow tired of it.

Until the incident with Pete.

She'd half decided she would leave after this month was over, but Pete had showed her a new side of him yesterday. If he could remain friendly, not aggressive or impatient, perhaps she could stay. Perhaps…

By six-thirty, when the men came in, Mary Jo had dinner ready. She gave them fifteen minutes to shower before she put dinner on the table.

"Perfect timing," Pete said as he entered the kitchen in clean jeans and a western shirt that brought out the gold flecks in his brown eyes.

"Thanks for the lunch today, Mary Jo," Hank said when he came in.

She smiled. "You're welcome. Did I pack enough for you?"

"Yes, it was great."

"Good. I hope dinner will please you as much."

"Mary Jo, you don't have to work so hard to make us happy," Pete interjected. "You know we'll eat almost anything."

She laughed. "I know, but I'm trying out recipes for the winter. I don't think I've fixed lasagna before."

"You made lasagna for tonight? That's one of my favorites!"

"Mine, too," Hank stated. "Good job, Mary Jo!"

The brothers ate enthusiastically, and each sat back with a sigh after he'd finished.

"Ready for dessert?" she asked. "I baked a cobbler."

"Wow, Mary Jo, I think I love you," Hank exclaimed. He received a ferocious frown from his brother.

"He didn't mean that, Mary Jo. But we're delighted you made a dessert."

"Thank you, both of you. I'll just clear the dishes—"

"No, we can do that. You get the dessert," Pete exclaimed, and nudged his brother into action. Both men got up immediately, and by the time Mary Jo returned with the cobbler à la mode, they were done.

They lingered over dessert, talking, until Pete sighed and patted his taut stomach. "I love your cobblers. I'd ask for another serving, but I'm way too full."

"I'm glad," Mary Jo replied. "I'll clean up—"

Pete stopped her. "No. The least we can do is the dishes."

"But—"

"We'll manage. You sit here and relax."

Mary Jo did sit back as the men worked. She could get used to this, she thought.

Maybe she would stay, after all.

THE NEXT DAY, when she was trying out a new recipe for cookies, Cliff brought up the same issue. "You know, Mary Jo, these new recipes of yours would work better if you're here to cook them next season."

She ducked her head. "I'm not sure, Cliff."

"Where would you get another job that you enjoy like this one? And have four months off?"

"Actually, there are a few."

"I know, but—but it's beautiful here. And you'll have four months off next year. It's one of the perks of working at a dude ranch, where the tourists aren't here all year round."

"I know, but..." Mary Jo looked up at the old man. "I want to stay here, but—"

"I guarantee Pete won't bother you. Just say you'll stay. If at any time he does something you don't like, I'll pull him back, I promise."

After a moment, she said, "I'll stay as long as Pete doesn't get too close."

"Oh, good, glad to hear that. I have to admit I've been worried about approaching you regarding the winter session."

"I'm thinking I'll stay for another year. I really like it here and Pete has been...nicer since the summer season ended."

"I don't know what was wrong with the

boy, but I'm glad you two are getting along okay now."

"We're getting along, Cliff, but that's all."

"I understand, Mary Jo. If you have any trouble with him, just tell me."

"Thank you. So, have you heard from Jessica and Jim?"

"Nah! They're so wrapped up in each other it was a relief to send them on their way."

"I know." She sighed. "It's nice to see someone so much in love."

"Hey, me and Leslie do a pretty good job, too."

Mary Jo grinned. "Yes, you do! When are you taking your honeymoon?"

"November. But now that we have our own house, it's almost like being on a honeymoon!"

"Yes, I think you're right."

Cliff was getting ready to leave when Mary Jo stopped him. "Would you like to take some cookies home with you?"

"You got extra?"

She smiled at him. "For you I do."

"Then bag 'em up, little lady."

Laughing, she did just that and handed the sack to Cliff.

"This is why we can't lose you, Mary Jo. Nobody bakes like you."

When Cliff went on his way, Mary Jo thought about the extra time she had these days. Maybe she should invite Leslie and him over for lunch one day a week. They could talk about activities they wanted to plan for guests who wouldn't be going skiing.

Of course, when Jessica and Jim got back, Mary Jo would have company again. But wasn't she going to take some time off in November? She'd planned to go home to see her folks. They lived only a couple of hours from here, in Wyoming. She'd seen them several times during the summer on her days off, which was as much as she had when she was in college.

She owed her parents a lot. They'd taught her all the techniques of running a café and her mother had taught her to cook. But somehow Mary Jo didn't feel so enthusiastic about going home anymore.

Rock River, Wyoming, wasn't very exciting, she thought with a sigh.

Not as exciting as, say, the time Jessica and Jim were having on their honeymoon.

Mary Jo wanted to have someone to share her life with, like Jessica had. But that was the problem she'd had with Pete. She'd been so eager for attention and male companionship that she'd tumbled into bed with him too soon.

She wasn't going to do that again! No matter what he offered. Her heart might have urged her to sleep with him, but her mind was in charge now. She wasn't going to trust a man who'd betrayed her. A man who thought he could take whatever was offered without having to commit.

Only, her heart wouldn't stay silent. And she couldn't resist Pete's charm. So she'd just have to avoid him.

Maybe she could go to France to the Cordon Bleu school and take a short course. That would be fun. Tonight, she'd do a search on her computer.

Breathing a sigh of relief, she began mixing the dough for another batch of cookies.

Now that her mind was settled, she could concentrate on baking.

Two hours later, the cookies had turned out well, and she was eating a late lunch. She hadn't decided what to make for dinner. Something that would bring smiles to Hank and Pete's faces—but only because appreciation for her cooking made her feel good.

After flipping through one of her favorite cookbooks, she found a chicken dish she hadn't tried. Once she'd prepared it and put it in the refrigerator, she picked up the phone and invited Leslie for lunch one day that week, telling her to bring Cliff along.

"That would be great, Mary Jo. I've missed seeing you since we ended the season."

"Me, too. The boys aren't much for companionship when they come in, after spending all day in the saddle."

"I bet that's true. Cliff has been wondering how they're doing."

"I think pretty well. We got caught out in the snowstorm Sunday evening, but they got us back home about nine-thirty."

"Oh, my, and we didn't even know!"

"It's all right. The guys found us shelter, built a fire, and brought me back when the storm ended."

"I'm glad they took care of you. But the three of you should inform us if you're all going out."

"I don't expect we will be anymore. But I may ride on Wednesdays if there's some-one free to go with me. Would you like to ride with me?"

"You know, that's a good idea. Maybe Cliff could come, too."

"That's fine with me."

"I'm so glad you called, Mary Jo. How about we come for lunch tomorrow and then go riding?"

"That sounds wonderful."

Mary Jo smiled. Seems she'd found the companionship she'd been looking for. And it didn't involve Pete. Then why wasn't she happy?

Chapter Three

Mary Jo's decision to try out new menu items for the winter session had encouraged Pete. Not that he had any hope of convincing her to consider him again as a romantic possibility. But he definitely wanted her to stay to cook for the ranch's guests. At least that's what he told himself.

He'd been watching his brother the last few days, wondering if Hank had any interest in Mary Jo. Her sparkling blue eyes and shining chestnut-brown hair would attract any man. But it seemed Hank's interest in her was strictly platonic.

Pete didn't believe his brother was serious about any woman yet. He was too young.

Of course, Pete was only three years older, but he'd learned a hard lesson this year. Since he would turn thirty in a month, he guessed it was time to get serious about life and about starting a family. Especially with the deaths of their parents in a car accident about nine months ago.

"Hey, Pete! Where's your mind? Get those cows back in the herd!"

Hank's deep voice carried across the hillside to him, startling Pete out of his reverie. He waved his hand and rode after the six cows that had wandered off.

Rounding up cattle was a lot easier than rounding up his thoughts!

WHEN LESLIE ARRIVED, Mary Jo greeted her with a warm hug. She liked the older woman and was glad about her marriage to Cliff. A widow with two sons living in other states, Leslie loved it here in Colorado and didn't want to move away.

She'd started working on the ranch as a receptionist, so Jessica could mingle more with the guests in order to, as Jim had put it, recognize any problems before they got worse. It had taken Jessica a little while to appreciate Leslie, but the older woman had soon won her over.

"How are you doing, Mary Jo?" Leslie asked now as she took off her coat.

"I'm fine. A little bored with my own company, actually. I'm grateful you agreed to come to lunch."

"We always look forward to your cooking," she said. "Cliff didn't even want to eat breakfast, since we were coming here for lunch but I threatened not to cook for him ever again if he didn't!"

"That's the way to handle a man," Mary Jo agreed with a laugh.

Cliff had stepped into the next room to check something, and returned in time to hear that last statement. "What are you talking about?" he asked suspiciously.

"We were just discussing how to, um, handle things."

"Okay. Well, are we ready to eat?"

"We are," Mary Jo replied. "Are you hungry?"

"Sure am. But I wanted to ask you about the boys."

Leslie had sat down at the table and was staring intently at her empty plate.

"Do you mean Pete and Hank, or all the cowboys?" Mary Jo inquired.

"Just Pete and Hank," Cliff said.

"They seem to be doing well. The last couple of days, since the storm, they've been bringing the herds down to the lowest pastures. Most of the snow has melted and they don't think they've lost any cows."

"Oh, good. I wondered about the losses."

"I didn't ask them last night, but they seemed to be in a good mood."

"Maybe that was because they were eating one of your delicious meals," Leslie suggested with a smile.

"I doubt it." She turned back to Cliff. "Do you want one of the boys to call you tonight?"

He sat down at the table. "That might be a good idea, Mary Jo. I miss seeing them all the time, I'll admit, and I want to check on the status of the herd."

"I'm sure they'll be glad to let you know how things are going."

"Good. Now, what are we having for lunch?"

Mary Jo brought out a quiche lorraine from the oven and a tossed salad from the refrigerator. Then she took some rolls from another oven.

As they started eating, she introduced the subject she wanted to talk about with Leslie. "Have you given much thought to activities we could offer winter guests if some of them don't go skiing?"

Her friend immediately gave her several suggestions, from snowshoeing to afternoon movie screenings.

"Oh, those sound good, Leslie. Why don't you start a list? I don't have a lot of time during a season, but I thought I might be able to offer a cooking lesson or two, if anyone would be interested. Maybe even a cookie-making session one afternoon, for kids."

"I like that idea, Mary Jo," Cliff said.

"I do, too," Leslie declared. "Especially if I get to help, so I can learn how to make those cookies you sent home with Cliff."

"I can give you the recipe, Leslie. I don't think you'd have any trouble with it."

"I appreciate your faith in me," her friend said with a chuckle.

"I'd like another piece of quiche…unless you're saving the rest for dinner tonight."

"No, Cliff, I don't think the guys would appreciate quiche for supper."

"Well, then, I'll have some more. It sure tastes good."

"Thank you."

"Are you having any trouble with Pete?" Cliff suddenly asked, staring at Mary Jo.

She dropped her gaze. "No, not at all. Both he and Hank have been well behaved and cooperative."

"I'm glad to hear it. I've got a plan for Pete, since he's the oldest," Cliff proclaimed.

Mary Jo looked at him. "What plan is that?"

"I've found him a lady."

"A lady?" Mary Jo's lips were dry and she felt a catch in her throat.

"Yeah, a woman in Steamboat Springs. I

figured if he was looking to date, he'd want somebody close by. And she's a looker."

"How…nice." Mary Jo kept her gaze down.

"Mary Jo, are you all right with—with everything?" Leslie asked.

"Oh, yes, of course. Everything's fine."

"Yeah, this little girl will put that boy through his paces," Cliff continued.

"I think we need to finish up lunch, dear," Leslie stated, obviously trying to change the subject.

"I think I might be interested in dessert," he said, smiling at Mary Jo.

"Of course. There's some crumb cake I baked yesterday. It will just take a minute."

As she served it, he continued to talk about his "plan." "I think the little lady I've picked out will have Pete not knowing which way he's going when he sees her. She's really hot."

"Cliff!" Leslie said sharply.

"Isn't that what they call girls these days?" he pressed.

"Yes, it is," Mary Jo said, making an effort to smile at him. “I’m sure Pete will be pleased.”

“Well, she promised to call him tonight, so you be sure he answers the phone.”

Mary Jo dipped her head behind the refrigerator door so Cliff couldn’t see her face. “I’ll try.”

“That’s not Mary Jo’s job, Cliff,” Leslie protested. “She’s the cook, not the babysitter!”

Mary Jo returned to the table with dessert. “Have you thought about doing some shopping for bingo prizes during the off time?” she asked Leslie.

“No, but that’s a good idea. We should build up a stock so we wouldn’t have to run to town every week.”

“I can help you while the guys are out riding. I don’t have a lot to do.”

“Just as long as you keep cooking, Mary Jo,” Cliff said. “You’re really good at it.” He forked up the last of his cake and looked up at her. “You know, these young men are missing the mark. I mean, you’re good-looking, too. You’d be a fine catch for some man.”

Mary Jo ducked her head yet again, and Leslie hit Cliff's arm.

"What? What did I say wrong?" he asked.

"Never mind. Let's go saddle up the horses for our ride."

PETE WAS SURE OF IT.

Mary Jo was avoiding him again. All through dinner she'd evaded his gaze, making him wonder if he'd upset her. He didn't think complimenting her cooking would put her in such a mood. "Is anything wrong, Mary Jo?"

"No, not at all." She didn't look at him then, either. "Oh! I almost forgot. Your grandfather wants one of you to call him this evening."

Pete and Hank looked at each other. Finally, Pete said, "You call Granddad, Hank. I talked to him last."

"Okay," he agreed with a hangdog air.

Mary Jo got up quickly, and Pete wondered again if something was bothering her. "Are you sure nothing is wrong?" he asked when she came back to the table with dessert.

"I'm sure. Will you pass me your plate?"

"Sure." After they'd eaten some delicious chocolate pie, he carried his plate and Hank's to the sink, but didn't notice any appreciation in her eyes. When the phone rang, he didn't even move, until Mary Jo asked him to answer it.

"Okay, maybe it's our sister calling to tell us she's having a good time on her honeymoon," he said with a grin. "Hello?"

He noticed Mary Jo watching him out of the corner of her eye. What was with her?

"No, I'm a little tired tonight. You want to talk to my brother? He has a tad more energy than me. Just a minute."

He turned to Hank. "You interested in going into town tonight?"

Hank eagerly moved to take the phone. His agreement to whatever the young woman was asking was immediate. Hanging up a minute later, he said, "I need to hurry up and get to town. There are some pretty ladies waiting for me."

"Weren't you going to call Granddad?" Pete asked.

"Can't you do it?"

"I guess, but you owe me."

Hank gave his brother a grin and ran out of the kitchen. Mary Jo heard him yell, "Thanks for dinner!"

"Are you sure you don't want to go into town with Hank?" she asked Pete.

"Nope. Not interested. I thought we might look at some of those movies Jessie bought and asked us to check out."

"We?"

"I thought you might join me. You know more what Jessie is looking for than I do."

Mary Jo seemed surprised; she stared at him before she said, "I suppose I could watch one with you. Just to rate it for Jessica."

"Of course. We'll set it up in the living room, just like a regular movie night."

"Okay. What are our choices?"

He rattled off five different movies—four romantic comedies and an action adventure. To his surprise, she chose the action movie.

"Are you sure?" he asked, eyeing her closely. "I thought you'd pick another one."

"No, that's the one I want to see." Another lie, Mary Jo thought. But how could she watch a romantic movie while alone in the house with Pete? She didn't want him to get any ideas, after all.

"Okay, fine, but we have to have popcorn."

"After that huge meal you ate?"

"Come on, Mary Jo, you can't watch a movie without popcorn."

"All right, all right, you win. I'm fixing popcorn."

"Thanks, honey. That will make it like a real movie show."

Pete took down a bowl for the popcorn as she put a bag in the microwave.

"You want a drink to go with it?" he asked.

"Make it a diet soda for me."

His eyes raked her slowly from head to toe, lingering on the curves of her breasts and thighs. "I don't know why," he said, a smile shimmering on his mouth. "You don't need to watch your figure."

She swatted him playfully. “Pete! Just get me the soda.”

“Whatever you want.”

He went to get the movie ready, and when Mary Jo arrived, she found one of the couches pulled up in front of the television. *Awfully cozy,* she thought.

“I think I’ll sit in a chair,” she announced.

In a low voice, Pete said, “Don’t do that, Mary Jo. I’m not going to attack you, I promise.”

“Pete, I can’t—”

“Besides, we can’t share the popcorn if you sit over there.”

Mary Jo drew a deep breath. Then she nodded and sat down on the couch. She could do this. She could sit next to Pete and not be tempted. He set the popcorn between them and passed her her soda. But when he jumped up and turned down the overhead light, casting the room in shadow, she felt herself on alert. Her body stiffened and she scooted away a couple of inches. Just in case.

Two hours later, the movie ended. The

popcorn was gone, and nothing had happened.

Pete got up and turned off the DVD. "What did you think of it?"

"I don't think it was PG rated. Too much violence."

"There are lots of violent movies made these days, it seems."

"But, Pete, you can't show that film to a bunch of kids. Their mothers will get upset."

"I guess you're right. Too bad. I really liked it."

"You can watch it during the vacation weeks, with Hank."

"Or you."

"No, I just saw it with you."

"Want to see another movie?"

"Are you sleeping in in the morning?"

"No, are you?"

"Of course not. I have to get up to fix your breakfast."

"Okay, let's go to bed."

She wanted to watch him squirm and stutter again, like the last time he'd said that, but she didn't have the heart. "Alone," she said. "We'll go to bed alone."

"That's what I meant. Alone."

Just as the two of them were heading for the kitchen, she heard a noise at the front door. "Who could that be?" she asked.

"I'll go see. It's probably Hank."

Mary Jo hurried to the kitchen. She hoped to get to bed before Hank came in. She didn't want to hear about the "hot" lady he'd met in Steamboat Springs.

Unfortunately, she got even more than a recap; she got the real thing. Hank came into the kitchen with not one woman but two who fell into the "hot" category.

"Hey, Mary Jo, can you rustle us up a snack?" he asked breezily as he led them to the table.

Mary Jo cut the last of the pie for them. "When you finish, if you'll just put your dishes in the sink, I'd appreciate it," she stated.

Pete came into the kitchen just then. "Why are they eating the rest of the pie?"

"Hank asked for a snack for his friends," Mary Jo whispered.

"You shouldn't be waiting on them. I'll speak to Hank."

"Pete, I asked them to put their dishes in the sink. I can take it from there. It's all right."

"No, it's not," he whispered back. "Where are you going?"

"To bed. Good night." Mary Jo moved past him toward the row of bedrooms behind the kitchen, reserved for staff.

"Good night. I'm going to have a word with Hank before I come to bed. Sweet dreams," he said, leaning toward her.

Mary Jo pulled away. She didn't know if he was trying to kiss her good-night or not, but she wasn't cooperating. She pushed past him and didn't stop until she'd shut her bedroom door behind her.

PETE WATCHED MARY JO scurry off to bed. With a sigh, he went to Hank and asked to talk to him for a minute, leading him a discreet distance from his guests. "You shouldn't have asked Mary Jo to fix something for you," he told his brother.

"Why not? She's supposed to be cooking for us."

"Yeah, for us, not for them." He nodded toward the women.

Hank smiled as he followed his brother's gaze. "These fine ladies are my guests. Why don't you join us?"

The two women were attractive, tall, slender and fit. The blonde looked over and smiled at Pete, while the redhead waved. Still, he declined the invitation. "No thanks, Hank. And be sure and clean up like Mary Jo asked."

He walked past the ladies, toward his room, snorting at the irony. The only woman he wanted was one who wouldn't have him.

Chapter Four

Mary Jo came to an abrupt halt when she stepped into the kitchen the next morning. The dishes from Hank's snack last night remained on the table.

Anger rose in her, but with a sigh she moved forward to clean up before she began breakfast. Just as she took a step toward the table, Pete came into the kitchen.

"Stop! You will not clean up after Hank and his friends."

"But—"

He held up a hand. "Just start breakfast. Hank will be cleaning up this mess." He disappeared down the hall.

Mary Jo stood there trying to decide what to do. She could clean the table in a few minutes. But Pete was a Ledbetter, and as such, he was her employer.

Before she could make up her mind, he dragged his brother into the kitchen. "Tell her," he demanded.

Looking embarrassed, Hank said, "I apologize, Mary Jo. I intended to put the dishes in the sink, but I was so tired when they finally left, I thought I'd get up and do it before you came in. Only, I overslept."

Mary Jo could believe that last part. Hank was dressed in his jeans and T-shirt, and he hadn't shaved. But she wasn't sure she believed he'd intended to do as she'd asked.

"Thank you, Hank," she murmured.

At Pete's order, Hank cleared the table and carried the dishes to the sink. But Pete didn't let him stop there.

"Rinse them and put them in the dishwasher," he told him.

"That's not necessary," Mary Jo protested.

"Yes, it is. Do you need any help with breakfast?" Pete asked.

She was surprised by his question. "No, of course not."

In no time she had blueberry pancakes

on the table. Pete had poured the coffee and set out the plates.

Hank slid into his chair, a stubborn look on his face. He picked up his coffee and took a sip. "Did you call Granddad last night?" he asked his brother.

"No, I didn't get around to it," Pete said.

"Then you're as bad as me!"

"Maybe I forgot, but I didn't leave work for you to do. I'll call him while we're riding out. He'll be up by then."

They ate silently after that, neither man speaking to the other. When Hank finished, he stood and said, "Thank you, Mary Jo. The pancakes were very good. I guess you didn't have time to fix us lunches, but that's okay."

"Yes, I did, yesterday afternoon. They're in the fridge."

"Oh. Thank you." He opened the refrigerator and took out two paper bags. He put Pete's by his plate and walked out of the kitchen.

"I think you upset Hank, Pete. It wasn't necessary to embarrass him so."

"Yes, it was. He needs to show you some respect."

Mary Jo nodded. Pete was certainly treating her with respect lately, she thought. He was helpful, considerate and true to his hands-off promise. It was a new side to his personality.

One she could fall for.

WHEN PETE GOT TO the barn, he found his brother sitting on his horse. Hank hadn't saddled Pete's mount, but Pete hadn't expected him to. He brought in his horse and started the process.

"I've been thinking," Hank began.

"Yes?" Pete said, surprised that his brother was speaking to him.

"I don't see any need for both of us to ride out every day unless we have really bad weather. Why don't we split the week? I'll be in charge Monday through Wednesday, and you can take over Thursday through Saturday. And we'll both be off on Sunday. That way we get some vacation, too."

Pete thought about that proposition. "You think it would work?"

"Yeah. And we could divide up the cowboys, so they get some time off, too."

"I'll ask Granddad when I call him. If he agrees, we'll start Monday."

"I don't see why we can't start at once. Then if I want to go to town tonight, I can come back late."

"I thought we could take Mary Jo to town for dinner tonight."

"We?"

"Yeah, to make up for your behavior!"

"I did the dishes!"

"Yeah, because I dragged you out of bed!"

"Fine! We'll take her to dinner. But that doesn't mean I'll have to come back early. So we'll drive into town separately."

"Fine!"

MARY JO WAS DECIDING WHAT to prepare for dinner when the phone rang. With a frown, she picked it up, wondering who was calling.

It was Pete.

He never phoned, and her body went on alert. "What's wrong?"

"Nothing. Hank and I want to take you out for dinner tonight."

She let out a breath. "Why?"

"Just for a nice break for you. We thought it might be fun."

"Pete, if you want to eat out tonight, that's fine. You don't have to take me with—"

"No, Mary Jo. I insist you go with us."

"Fine!"

Pete was certainly getting used to being the boss.

A COUPLE OF HOURS LATER, after taking a break, Pete stood up and flipped his phone closed. His grandfather had sure acted funny during their conversation. He kept asking how his night in town had gone. If he'd met anyone special. Pete had told him he was confusing him with Hank, but Cliff didn't get it.

Usually his grandfather was sharp as a barbwire fence. Odd…

He mounted and met up with Hank.

"Granddad agreed with your plan. But I think we need to add something to it."

"What?" Hank asked sharply.

"When you work, you cook your own breakfast. We can both do that, and that means Mary Jo can have a little vacation, too."

Hank took a moment to consider that suggestion. "Okay, I'll agree to that."

"Good."

"But you're working tomorrow. Right?"

"Right."

Pete was glad their grandfather thought Hank's plan was a good one. Pete certainly looked forward to having the first half of the week off. Would Mary Jo like it? He could offer to help her do her work, whatever it was. Remembering some of the things Jim had done with Jessie gave him an idea. He could offer to go shopping for prizes for the bingo nights they put on for the guests. With Mary Jo, of course.

Would she trust him enough to go with him? He hoped so. It would be fun. And they'd get to know each other better. Before, he'd been too rushed to take time for important things like talking to her.

What else could he find to do with Mary Jo?

MARY JO HEARD THE MEN come in that night and knew she had a little more time to get ready, since they would immediately take showers.

All day she'd told herself not to get excited about the evening plans, but she still was looking forward to it—even if Pete wanted to see the "hot" women in town, as Cliff put it. Mary Jo hadn't been out to eat in a long time.

When someone knocked on her bedroom door, she drew a deep breath before she got up and answered it.

"Hi, Mary Jo. Are you ready?" Pete asked. He looked handsome, dressed in black slacks and a cranberry-colored shirt that emphasized his dark hair and eyes.

She nodded.

"Where's Hank?"

"He's going to drive his truck because

he may not want to come back right after supper."

"I can drive yours back if you want to stay late, too."

"I'll be ready to come back when you are. Besides, I have something to tell you about our schedule for October."

"Okay," she agreed, worried what he was going to say. Was he planning to tell her they didn't need her that month?

She'd have to admit she would miss working on the Lazy L, even for a few weeks. She laughed to herself. Obviously, she needed to get a life!

Stepping out into the hallway and closing her door, she turned to follow Pete, only to find him standing there.

"Did you forget something?" she asked, looking at him in surprise.

"Nope. I was just waiting for you."

They walked out together, which made Mary Jo nervous. His musky cologne filled her nostrils as she breathed, and she tried to move farther away from him.

"Anything wrong?" he asked.

"No. I—I was just thinking. It's unusual to go out for a meal. At least for me."

"I think you deserve to do something like that every once in a while. We take your cooking for granted."

They'd reached his truck and he opened the passenger door for her.

"Thank you," she said softly, smiling up at her chivalrous escort.

Once he started driving, she said, "What did you want to tell me?"

"We've decided to each take a vacation, Hank and me. Granddad approved it, too."

"Oh, so you're going away?" Why did she suddenly feel as if the luster was gone from her special evening?

"No. I mean, we'll split the week. There's no need for both of us to work every day, now that we've got the herds close by. So Hank will work Monday through Wednesday, and I'll work Thursday through Saturday. We'll both be off on Sunday."

"That will be nice for you."

"And whoever is working will fix his own breakfast, so you won't have to get up early at all."

"But that's my job!"

"You already do a lot, Mary Jo. And you're supposed to be having a rest, too. Until the winter season starts. Then we'll all get really busy again."

"No, I'm supposed to be providing your meals!"

"Just try it. You may get used to sleeping in. And you can still cook breakfast for whoever's off that day."

"We'll see."

They pulled into the parking lot of a nice restaurant, stopping beside Hank's truck. "He must've driven fast, to already be inside," Pete said.

Mary Jo remained silent. She still wasn't sure they were there for her enjoyment. Cliff's words kept echoing in her ears: *"The little lady I've picked out will have Pete not knowing which way he's going."*

He escorted her into the restaurant, looking for his brother. "There he is," Pete said, moving toward him.

Mary Jo followed Pete to the table and took the chair he held out for her. "Thank you," she murmured, and smiled at Hank.

"Pete told me about your new schedule. It sounds…interesting."

"I think it's great."

"You'd better. I had to talk Granddad around to it," Pete stated.

"You didn't tell me that earlier," Hank said.

He shrugged. "I didn't mind… Are you looking for someone?" he asked, when Hank kept glancing around.

Before he could answer, two women approached their table.

"Hank! We didn't know you were coming in tonight!"

Mary Jo's stomach fell. One of the two, a blonde, had been out at the ranch last night. She was obviously the one Cliff intended for Pete, because she walked up and slid her arm around his shoulders as he sat at the table. "Hello, there," she said, flashing a brilliant white smile. "Glad to see you've come to join us."

Mary Jo drew in a silent breath. She'd been expecting their arrival. She was prepared to return home as soon as Pete gave her his keys.

"I didn't," he replied to the blonde. "We're taking Mary Jo out to dinner."

"Then we'll join Mary Jo," she teased.

"I'm afraid we don't have room at this table for five people. Maybe another time."

The generous smile on the blonde's face disappeared. "Oh. Well, excuse us for interrupting." She flounced back to her table.

The other woman whispered something in Hank's ear and then left, too.

"I'm going to join them," Hank announced. "You don't mind, do you, Mary Jo?"

"Of course not. If Pete will give me his keys, I can drive his truck back and fix myself something for dinner at home."

Pete roared, "You'll do no such thing! We'll have dinner as planned…without Hank, of course."

"Pete, there's no reason to give up dinner with those two women just for me. I understand."

"I don't!" He collected himself and added, "I have to get up in the morning. Hank doesn't. So he can go entertain the ladies until all hours." He gestured to the place where his brother had stood a moment ago, but Hank was gone. "So I'll enjoy a nice meal with you and then go home for a good night's rest. Okay?"

"Yes, if that's what you want, but I really—"

"Enough, Mary Jo. You're stuck with me tonight."

She didn't protest again, but wondered what he was up to. She didn't think his decision would make him very popular with the blonde at the other table.

He opened his menu. "What are you going to have, Mary Jo?"

"I—I haven't decided."

"I think I'll have a steak tonight."

"I might have a salad."

"Come on, Mary Jo. You can do better than that. Why don't you have a steak, too?"

"Pete, will you let me pay for my dinner?"

"Of course not. I invited you."

"No, actually you *ordered* me to come out to dinner. Let me pay for my meal."

"Absolutely not."

Mary Jo heaved a sigh and Pete shot her a glance. “Are you all right?”

“Yes, but I don’t see why you’re being so difficult.”

PETE WISHED HE COULD TELL her. He didn’t like to keep anything back, but he knew she wouldn’t want to hear that he enjoyed spending time with her. It would spook her again, and he couldn’t take the chance.

The waitress came to take their orders, and they both asked for steak. Her timing was impeccable, as it gave Mary Jo a chance to cool down.

When the server left, they sat in silence for a few moments. There were so many things Pete wanted to say to Mary Jo, so much he wanted to talk about, but he was afraid to upset her. He settled on something innocuous. “I like the music they’re playing.”

“You like rock?” she asked in surprise. “I thought you preferred country and western.”

“Some of it. Not all of it.”

"I guess we didn't…I mean, I don't think we've talked about music before."

"No, we didn't talk about anything before— That is, I guess we haven't had a chance to talk about a lot of things." He tried not to remember what they'd done the one night when they'd been together. He tried not to recall how she felt in his arms, how she sighed as he kissed her. Their attraction had been instant, mutual, volatile, and in no time he'd made love to her. They hadn't taken time to get to know each other.

He wouldn't make that mistake again.

Chapter Five

They talked about everything. Over drinks and dinner they shared easy conversation about what it was like to grow up as the eldest sibling, about ranch life in Colorado versus a small Wyoming town. About their favorite foods, favorite family vacations, favorite memories.

For the first time Pete felt he was getting to know the woman he'd made love to during the summer. Not the curve of her hip, the small of her back. The real woman.

He fell for her all over again.

Hard.

Not wanting their time together to end, he offered to go to town with her to pick out bingo prizes on his days off.

"That's very nice of you, but Leslie offered to go with me."

"Couldn't I come, too? I don't mind Leslie being with us."

"If you want to, I suppose. But you might be bored with shopping."

"Jim went once with Jessie, so it must not be too bad. And I think you need a guy to choose some of the men's prizes."

"I don't know what time Leslie will want to go."

"That's okay. I'll have three days off. I can be flexible."

"All right, fine. I'll ask her tomorrow what day she'd like to do it."

"Okay. And then on Wednesday, after lunch, we can go for a ride."

"Yes, Leslie and Cliff enjoyed that this week. I think that will be fun."

"Oh. I didn't know they would go with us."

"Yes. So you don't have to come along, if you don't want to. I can imagine you'd be tired of riding."

Pete was getting a strong impression she didn't want to be with him. But he persisted. "No, I'll go with you. I can be the leader of our little troop."

"Maybe Cliff would like to be leader."

He couldn't help but sigh. This woman was tough.

When she finished her meal, Pete asked, "What do you think about dessert?"

"I couldn't. But don't let me stop you."

"No, I won't have any, either." But he didn't want to take her home and end the night, retiring to their separate bedrooms. "Do you want to dance a little? The band sounds good."

She didn't hesitate when she said, "No, but you can go join Hank. I'm sure the others would welcome you."

"You keep trying to get rid of me, sweetheart, but it's not going to work."

Her eyes flared right before she averted them. "You called me sweetheart. That's not…you said we could become friends again, not—not anything else."

"I'm sorry. I forgot." He couldn't explain his slip any other way that she would accept.

She was saved an explanation by the waitress. "How about dessert? We've got a chocolate brownie covered in ice cream and whipped cream, with a cherry on top. It's plenty for two people."

Pete looked at Mary Jo and read a no on her face. But the thought of sharing a dessert with her was just too tempting. "I think that sounds like a good idea. We'll take one."

"I guess you wanted dessert, after all," Mary Jo said when the woman left.

"I thought it might be fun to share. You can eat a little, can't you?"

"I'll have the cherry," she conceded.

"I hope you'll eat a bit more than that. Please?"

She didn't say anything, and Pete could only hope that she'd be won over once the treat was in front of them.

He started talking about his work that day, telling her about an ornery cow that didn't want to be herded. Maybe he embellished his story a little, but he was relieved when Mary Jo laughed. He came up with other stories to entertain her, all about the ranch. In the middle of one, their dessert arrived.

He waited until Mary Jo scooped off the

cherry and ate it. Then he dug into the ice cream and continued his tale.

She was a great listener. His dramatics kept her attention, and they both kept eating until the dessert was all gone.

"That was good, wasn't it?" he asked at last.

She appeared startled by the empty plate in front of them. "You tricked me, Pete Ledbetter! I didn't intend to eat any of it!"

"Well, we both sinned together. That makes it all right, doesn't it?"

"I doubt it. You never look like you gain any weight. But those calories will settle on my hips!"

"Your hips look pretty good from here, sweetheart," he said, as he gave her a once-over.

Her face flared a bright red before she seemed to catch herself. Then she chastised him. "Pete, I'm serious. You must stop calling me that. You said we'd be friends—just friends."

"Sorry. It, uh, I forgot." What else could he say?

The waitress brought their bill and he

offered his credit card. When he'd signed the slip, he turned to Mary Jo. "Are you ready to go?"

"Yes, but are you sure you don't want to stay?"

"Only if you'll dance with me."

She shook her head. "I'm ready to go home, if you are. I think we've played hooky long enough."

He grinned at her. "I kind of like playing hooky. After all, Jessie and Jim are taking the entire month off."

"And Cliff and Leslie are going away next month."

"Yeah. It almost makes you want—Never mind." Bad idea. If he'd completed his sentence, she'd run away for sure. *It almost makes you want to get married so you can have a honeymoon.*

He helped her with her coat and then escorted her out of the restaurant.

"Did you tell Hank goodbye?" she suddenly asked.

"No, honey. But he won't miss me, I promise."

"You can't call me honey, either, Pete."

"I call a lot of women honey. It doesn't mean anything." He hoped that excuse would work.

"I don't want to be part of your 'women,' Pete! That's the problem we had in the first place, wasn't it?"

"Mary Jo—"

"Never mind. I don't want to talk about it!"

He opened the passenger door of his truck and waited until she was settled in her seat. Then he circled the vehicle and joined her inside. "You warm enough?"

"Yes, thank you." She stared straight ahead, refusing to look at him.

He couldn't think of any more conversation to amuse her. He was too depressed. If only he could reach over and pull her into his arms. Or even reach out and hold her hand. But he didn't think either action would be welcome.

"Mary Jo, I wasn't trying to... You looked so adorable, I forgot. Will you forgive me?"

"Yes, of course."

He didn't believe her.

PETE SET OUT EARLY in the morning. They were riding fence lines on the lower pastures to be sure there wouldn't be any cattle straying and getting into trouble. Most of the snow from the past weekend had melted so the cattle could still find some grass to eat.

He wished he could rein in his thoughts as efficiently. But they kept straying back to Mary Jo. Ever since they'd gotten caught in the storm last Sunday, things had been better between Mary Jo and him. If only he hadn't upset her last night by calling her sweetheart. But she was so darn cute! He smiled as he thought about how pretty she'd looked.

Damn, he'd messed up so badly last summer.

And now he was paying a terrible price.

MARY JO STAYED IN HER room until she heard Pete leave the house. She waited another five minutes before she tiptoed into the kitchen. Then she stopped short.

He had cleaned the entire room after breakfast. She hadn't expected that. Smiling, she admitted it was the nicest thing he'd ever done.

Mary Jo stood there, thinking about all the kind gestures Pete had made lately. Taking her riding, to dinner, being considerate of her time. He seemed like…a different man. She caught herself before she could take that thought further.

She fixed herself some breakfast and then ate it, lingering over a second cup of coffee. This was nice once in a while, but she longed to be making meals for guests again. Cooking was her passion as well as her job. Maybe because she'd grown up cooking at home, in the family-owned café. She still did when she went back to visit.

Because she had the time today, she decided to experiment on a French recipe she'd been wanting to try out. It was complicated, but she was up for a challenge.

She'd just finished reducing the brandy sauce when Hank stumbled into the kitchen. "Something smells good."

"Thank you, Hank. That's dinner tonight."

"I didn't sleep that late, did I?" he asked, looking confused.

Mary Jo laughed. "No, of course not. Come on," she said, leading him to the table. "I'll make some pancakes for you."

"That would be nice. And I could use a cup of coffee—and some aspirin, too."

She didn't comment on his request, just brought him the coffee and medication.

By the time she had the casserole in the refrigerator and Hank was finished with his breakfast, the coffee and the aspirin seemed to have brought him back to life.

"Did you have fun last night?" Mary Jo asked him.

He looked up. "Yeah, it was great. We shut the place down. I'm sorry Pete didn't stay."

"I offered to drive his truck back here for him, but he refused. He acted like he thought I would wreck it!"

"Maybe he'll stay tonight," Hank said.

"You're going back into town tonight?"

He grinned. "Yeah. I'm liking this new schedule we've got. I intend to go out every night I can."

Mary Jo turned away. She didn't want him to see the disappointment on her face. Because she knew sooner or later his brother would join him.

PETE WAS STARVING by the time he reached the barn that evening. Going without lunch after he'd gotten used to having it wasn't fun.

But it was his fault. He could've fixed himself some sandwiches that morning. That wouldn't have been as good as Mary Jo's lunches, but at least he would've had something.

As he unsaddled his horse, he told himself he needed self-discipline. He needed to forget his hunger. And to forget his hunger to see Mary Jo, too. There'd be no calling her sweet names, no matter what she did. No kissing her. No touching.

After he took care of his horse, he walked slowly to the house, repeating his warnings with each step.

When he opened the back door, warmth surrounded him. A moment later Mary Jo appeared.

"Are you frozen and starved to death?" she asked with a sympathetic smile.

"No, I'm fine," he assured her.

"I bet you're ready to eat," she stated.

"Sure. Is supper ready?"

"Almost. It needs fifteen more minutes in the oven, so you have time for a shower."

He wanted so badly to sweep her up in his arms and kiss her sweet lips. But that would be a big mistake.

"Okay, I'll go have one."

"We'll be waiting for you."

As she turned back toward the kitchen, he stared at her curvy figure. If he could only… No, no way. She'd hate him forever if he even touched her.

With a sigh, he headed for his room. At least one of his hungers could be fulfilled tonight. He should be grateful for that.

MARY JO WAS TAKING dinner out of the oven when Pete returned.

"Perfect timing," she said, tossing a smile over her shoulder. "The casserole's ready."

"What kind of casserole?" he asked.

"A special one, since I forgot to make you a lunch."

He smiled back at her. "Don't worry about it. I could've grabbed something, but I forgot, too."

"Well, I hope this will make up for it," she said. Having placed the casserole on the table, she invited Pete to sit down.

He discovered his brother had taken the only seat on the right side of the table, leaving him to sit on the other side with Mary Jo.

He could've kissed Hank.

But he'd rather kiss Mary Jo.

Reminding himself of his warnings earlier, Pete sat down and focused on the food. He waited for her to sit beside him, then took his first bite. "This is really good!"

"I'm glad you like it," she said with enthusiasm.

"In fact, Mary Jo, you've really outdone yourself."

"It's not a type of dish I could cook often. This cut of meat costs too much and the dish takes too long to prepare. But for special occasions, I think French cuisine is great," she said with a smile.

Pete couldn't help himself. She looked so proud of herself, he leaned in and kissed her soft lips. His appetite for food disappeared and he lost himself in the moment. He'd swear Mary Jo was lost in the kiss, too, but then she yanked away from him, looking shocked.

"Pete, you can't— Don't do that!" she cried.

He grimaced. "I wasn't going to, but you looked so pleased with yourself, I couldn't help it."

"Come on, Mary Jo," Hank said. "He was just congratulating you on making a great dinner. I'm sure that's all he was doing."

Pete sent his brother a grateful look for his support. But he knew it wouldn't satisfy Mary Jo.

"I promise I wasn't trying to start anything. I just wanted to congratulate you, like Hank said."

She got up from the table, in a huff. "Next time, a polite thank-you will do!"

"Won't you come sit back down?" Pete asked.

"I'm not hungry right now." She stomped out of the kitchen and went to her bedroom.

"Damn! Damn! Damn!" Pete sat there staring after her.

"Man, that wasn't smart!" Hank said. "She's a little sensitive right now. Why don't you get a girlfriend? One of the gals I've been hanging out with thinks you're pretty cool. I could—"

"No! I don't want anyone else. I'm—I'm trying to make Mary Jo comfortable here. I want her to stay."

"Well, you're sure not going to do it by kissing her! That will make her leave and not even finish the month! You'd better watch what you're doing."

"I know that!" Pete yelled.

"Well, damn it, then why are you kissing her?"

"Just eat your meal, Hank."

"Okay. It's really great."

"I know."

Hank continued eating for several minutes before he realized Pete was just sitting there. "Why aren't you eating?"

"I'm not in the mood."

"Man, you didn't even have any lunch today! Are you crazy?"

"Yeah, I think I am," Pete said sadly.

"I can't believe you're not starving! You're turning into a girl! We've always been able to eat no matter what!"

"Maybe I'm getting old," Pete said with a sigh. He began covering the serving dishes to put in the refrigerator.

He wished his sister was here. Female advice would come in handy right now. Hank wasn't any help. He could tell Pete what he'd done wrong, but not what he needed to do to make it right.

Should he go to her room? Or would that make it worse?

After Hank left, Pete cleaned up the kitchen and put the plates and cutlery in the dishwasher. Then he paced the floor, debating what he should do.

Suddenly he remembered there was another woman on the ranch. Leslie! He could ask her for advice.

He grabbed the phone and dialed the number for his grandfather's house.

"Uh, Granddad, is Leslie there?"

"Of course she's here, boy. Where else would she be?"

"Yeah, well, I need to talk to her."

"Why?"

"I—I have a problem and I need to ask her advice."

"Problem with what?"

"Granddad, I need to speak to Leslie!"

"I don't see why—"

"It's—it's about Mary Jo!"

"We'll be right over!" And the phone went dead.

Chapter Six

Pete sat with his head in his hands. He didn't know what to do now. He'd wanted to talk to Leslie alone. An impossibility, he knew.

Cliff and Leslie hurried into the kitchen.

Pete looked up and made the request anyway. "Granddad, I'd like to speak to Leslie by herself."

"Just tell us what you did, Pete!" Cliff bellowed. "There's no need to keep it a secret. Mary Jo will be leaving if we don't get things straightened out."

Leslie put a hand on her husband's arm. "Cliff, perhaps if you'd let me talk to Pete alone, it would be easier."

"No reason to make it easy for the boy! He's goofed up again."

Pete jumped in. "I—I kissed Mary Jo. It

wasn't… I mean, she was so proud of herself, I just felt… I wanted to congratulate her on something she was happy about. It was a natural response!"

Leslie looked at him sympathetically. "How did she react?"

"She stormed to her room, refusing to eat."

"Did you apologize?" Cliff demanded.

"Of course I did, Granddad!"

"Then what do you need Leslie for?"

Pete turned to her, exasperated. "I don't know what to do next. Should I go knock on her door? Apologize again? I don't want to do the wrong thing, Leslie. What do you think?"

"Let me go talk to her," she suggested.

MARY JO HAD SETTLED on her bed. Though she'd shed a few tears, she was composed now. At least she thought so. Then she heard a knock on her door. Panic filled her, until she heard a woman's voice.

"Mary Jo? It's Leslie. May I come in?"

Opening the door, she invited the older woman in.

"Are you all right?" Leslie murmured.

"Yes. Did Pete ask you to come?"

She nodded. "He's afraid he'll scare you away."

"Yes."

"Yes, he's scared you away? Oh, Mary Jo, don't go. I'd miss you so much."

"I know, but… I don't know what to do!"

"Do you want to stay on the ranch?"

"Of course I do, but Pete promised. He said we could become friends!"

"What do you want him to do? Should he apologize again?"

"No! No, I just need some time to… I'm not sure this is such a bright idea. I should've left when the season was over. At least when the dude ranch was filled with guests I was too busy to think."

"Please won't you try just a little longer?"

Mary Jo avoided Leslie's pleading glance. Staring at a poster she'd put on her wall when she'd first moved into the room, she thought back to her eager hopes of that day. After a moment, she looked at Leslie. "I probably reacted too much to his—his kiss. It *was* a congratulatory kiss. But it stirred up things I don't want to remember. If he could just—just give me some space, maybe things would work out."

"I'll talk to him. He's worried that you didn't eat dinner."

"Did he eat?"

"Pete? I don't know."

"I'm only going out there if he's left the kitchen."

"Okay. I'll make sure he's gone, then I'll come get you."

"Yes, please."

PETE KNEW HE'D ESCAPED a disaster. If Mary Jo left, his grandfather would blame him. Rightly so. So he vowed this time he would not do those things that irritated Mary Jo.

He'd asked Leslie to go with him and Mary Jo when they went shopping for gifts. She'd agreed to do so on Monday, which was fine with him. But now he had to get through Sunday.

Making sure his brother had gone to the kitchen before him, Pete went to breakfast.

"Good morning," he said to both Hank

and Mary Jo. Not making eye contact with either of them, he took his place at the table.

She immediately put a full plate in front of him and then one for Hank. But she didn't sit down herself.

Looking at her, he asked, "Have you already eaten?"

"I have," she replied, avoiding his gaze.

"Are you going to church this morning?"

"Yes."

"I thought I'd go, too."

She said nothing.

"Do you want a ride with me?"

"Thank you, but I'm driving with Cliff and Leslie."

"Maybe I should, too. We should save gas where we can. Hank, are you coming to church?"

"Nah. I'm doing some odd jobs around here."

Mary Jo looked at Pete and he shrugged.

THERE WAS LITTLE conversation on the way to church. Mary Jo rode in the back seat with Pete, but she kept her gaze fixed on the passing scenery. She felt odd dressed in stockings and heels and a skirt. She didn't have time for church during the season.

Pete was dressed up, too, and looked wonderful in his suit. She put a lot of effort into not staring at him. There would be plenty of women who did that when he appeared in church.

"Mary Jo, are you going to Sunday school first?" Leslie asked.

"Yes, I'd like to."

"Okay, I can show you the right place," she said with a smile.

Mary Jo thanked her. She felt Pete's gaze on her, but refused to acknowledge his attention. Going with Cliff and Leslie had seemed a brilliant idea when she'd come up with it, but Pete's decision to save gas, as if she believed that excuse, had made her uncomfortable.

Cliff turned into the parking lot of the church they attended. "After service, we'll go out to lunch. A reward for our dressing up," he added with a smile.

"But what about Hank?" Mary Jo asked.

She was responsible for preparing food for him, even lunch on Sunday.

"I'll call him when we decide where to go, and see if he wants to drive in to meet us. If he doesn't, he can manage by himself."

She said nothing. When she got out of Cliff's car, she drew a deep breath.

Pete immediately came around the vehicle to join her and Leslie. "I can show Mary Jo where to go. We're in the singles class, Leslie."

"I'm not sure—" Leslie began.

"I'll take care of her," he promised.

What was wrong with the man? Hadn't she made herself clear last night? Mary Jo shrugged her shoulders, accepting Pete's escort. It seemed silly for Leslie to go out of her way for no reason.

Sunday school was pleasant. Pete behaved himself and introduced her to a lot of people. But he stuck to her side like glue, blocking any hope of her mingling on her own.

They joined Cliff and Leslie for the church service, sliding into the pew where they were sitting. Mary Jo tried to concentrate on the sermon, but how could she with Pete pressed alongside her? She scooted over a bit, but moving did little good. The scent of his aftershave invaded her nostrils, making it nearly impossible to focus on anything but him.

She'd never wished more for the end of a service.

After church, Mary Jo would have preferred to go back to the ranch, where she could hide, but felt obliged to go along with Cliff's plan for eating out.

He picked one of the nicest restaurants in Steamboat Springs. It wasn't the same place she'd had dinner with Pete, which was a relief. At least she wouldn't expect to see the women who had come out to the ranch with Hank.

They went in and the hostess seated them. Leslie settled on a banquette, with Cliff across from her, which meant Mary Jo would sit across from Pete. That was certainly better than being seated beside him. She smiled at Cliff in gratitude.

"Why, Cliffie! I haven't seen you in

ages!" A young blonde threw herself at him, hugging his neck.

Leslie looked irritated. "Perhaps I should introduce myself," she said coldly. "I'm *Mrs.* Cliffie!"

"Oops, sorry about that, but Cliffie has always been a favorite fella of mine."

Since the blonde was practically sitting in his lap, Mary Jo didn't see how anyone could argue that. When the woman jumped up and ran to throw her arms around Pete, Mary Jo stiffened.

"I'm so glad to see you, too, Pete. You didn't come around much during the summer!"

"I was working."

"Hank showed up a lot more than you…" She smiled at him coyly, but then looked at Mary Jo. "Wait a minute. Don't tell me you're Mrs. Pete?"

"No, definitely not. If you'll excuse me, I need to powder my nose."

"I'll join you," Leslie said quickly, sliding out of her seat.

"But, Leslie—" Cliff tried to object, but

she ignored him, following Mary Jo across the restaurant.

"Little girl, I think you upset my wife. Don't do that again," he finally said, irritation on his face.

Pete immediately asked her to go away, not bothering with niceties. "We're taken. Find other men to try that clinging act on."

"But Cliff said you were available!" she said.

"He was wrong."

"Well, really!" she exclaimed, and walked away, muttering to herself.

"What did you do, Granddad? Set me up with any woman you could find?"

"You've got to get Mary Jo off the brain. She doesn't want anything to do with you. I thought finding someone else would help you."

"Don't help me, please. I'll find my own woman." Pete stood as Leslie and Mary Jo returned.

Cliff stood also, and pulled the table out a little so the women could slide onto the banquette.

"I see Little Miss Sunshine has disappeared," Leslie said icily. "I do hope she didn't think we were unfriendly."

"Sorry, sweetheart," Cliff said with an ingratiating smile.

Pete didn't say anything, but he was glad he'd gotten rid of the young woman. Just as he'd fended off the men in the singles class that morning when Mary Jo arrived. They'd sat up like dogs waiting for attention, but he'd made sure they were disappointed.

"Did you hang out here a lot before we married?" Leslie asked coolly.

"I didn't like to cook, honey," Cliff said.

"Obviously. I'm not sure you married me because you loved me. I think you just wanted someone in the kitchen!"

"Leslie, I'm sure that's not true," Mary Jo said hurriedly.

"No, sweetheart! Your cooking is wonderful, but I could've just stayed in the big house if that was what I wanted." Cliff reached out for her hand. "I love you and want to share my life with you."

Pete gazed earnestly at Leslie. "Granddad is so much happier since he married you. He's a very lucky man."

"Yes, I am, sweetheart." Cliff reached over and touched Leslie's cheek. When she leaned into his hand, Mary Jo knew she'd forgiven him.

Lunch at the restaurant, after having begun so poorly, was very enjoyable. Mary Jo even talked with Pete without feeling threatened. The only problem arose when he asked Leslie what time they'd be going shopping tomorrow.

"You're going shopping with Pete?" Cliff asked.

"Yes, we're going to buy some bingo prizes to store up so Jessica won't have to make a weekly trip to Steamboat Springs."

"I think I should come along," Cliff said at once.

"Granddad, I promise to bring her home safely. It'll be all right."

"You'd better make sure of that," he said sternly. "Hey, are you going, too, Mary Jo?"

"Yes, I think so."

"Well, I'd better stay at the ranch then. Hank might run into trouble."

PETE WOKE UP the next morning looking forward to his day. And it would start with breakfast with Mary Jo.

But when he reached the kitchen, he found it empty. He fixed himself bacon and eggs and toast, then ate alone, thinking of Mary Jo.

He knew she wouldn't pass up the shopping trip, as long as Leslie was going. Mary Jo wasn't the only one who was glad they had a chaperone. He stayed in better control with Leslie around.

With three hours to fill before the trip to town, he went to the barn. He could always polish some tack or make some repairs. That would keep him out of trouble until then.

When he returned to the kitchen a little before ten, having just showered, he found Mary Jo staring out the window. "Hi there. Are you ready for our trip to town?"

"I—I guess so. Have you seen Leslie?"

"No, but I'm sure she'll be here. While

we wait for her, do you have a few cookies? I'd enjoy a little snack."

"Yes, of course. Do you want a cup of coffee, too?"

"Yeah, that would be good." He sat down at the table when she put cookies on a plate for him. "Mmm, these hit the spot."

She didn't answer him, but picked up a cookie herself and munched on it. When they heard the back door open and saw Leslie walk in, both of them sighed in relief.

"Are you two ready?" she asked.

"Yeah, we are," Pete said, standing up and reaching for the rest of the cookies.

"I was afraid you'd forgotten," Mary Jo told her.

"No, I love shopping too much to pass up an opportunity to buy things without paying."

"Gee, you mean we don't have to pay?" Pete teased.

"Well, we do, but we're spending the ranch's money. That's more fun!" Leslie said with a smile. "Let's go."

The arrangement worked well for Pete.

He only offered his opinion when he thought something was an appropriate prize for a man. Otherwise, he followed along, carrying shopping bags, making occasional trips to the SUV to drop off packages, and returning to carry more.

He was able to watch Mary Jo enjoying herself. She was relaxed and looked as if she was having fun, something he hadn't seen much of the last few months.

Around noon, he called a halt and said they all had to eat. Both his companions agreed. Over lunch, Mary Jo even talked to him.

When they finally decided they had done enough damage, they got in the SUV and started for home. It had begun snowing, but not heavily, just a typical day in the mountains.

On the ride back, Pete decided he felt good about their outing. He figured he needed more normal activities like this to do with Mary Jo, so she'd be comfortable with him.

Suddenly she screamed, "Stop!"

He did so, then turned to see what was

wrong. She'd opened her door and was scrambling out into the snow. Pete immediately came around the truck, not sure what she was upset about. He followed her down to a mountain stream running alongside the road.

Then he saw what she had spotted: two puppies in the snow, so young their eyes were still closed.

Mary Jo picked up both puppies as Pete looked around. He hoped she didn't notice the three other puppies lying in the stream, obviously drowned.

But she did.

"Pete, we have to bury them. We can't leave them there!"

"I know, honey. I'll take care of it. Go ahead and get in the truck with those two pups."

In the back of the SUV he found an old feed sack and used it to take the drowned puppies out of the stream. People dumped unwanted animals sometimes, and he hated it. Trying to get rid of helpless puppies, so young they didn't have their eyes open yet, was doubly cruel.

When he got back in the truck, he saw that each of his passengers was holding a frozen puppy and trying to warm it.

"Were the others all dead?" Mary Jo asked softly.

"Yeah. You've got a good eye, seeing these two. You saved their lives. But I think we're going to have to feed them soon. I don't know how long they were out there."

"Do you think we can keep them alive?" Leslie asked.

"It depends on how fast you can warm them up and if they'll eat. What do we have to feed them?"

Mary Jo didn't hesitate. "I have canned milk. I think that will give them the best nutrients. We can heat it up for them."

"Okay. And we'll take them to the vet tomorrow if they get through the night."

"They'll probably have to be fed several times tonight." Leslie was stroking her puppy. "He's licking my hand."

"I know. Mine is, too. I'll get up a few times during the night to feed them."

Pete looked at Mary Jo out of the corner of his eye. "I'll get up, too. It will take two of us. But what if they don't drink out of a bowl? How will we feed them?"

"I think we could use eyedroppers, if we can find some."

"Cliff saves eyedroppers. We can take a couple of those. When we get home, I'll go get them while you heat up the milk," Leslie offered.

"Good. I fed a puppy when I was little. I think eyedroppers work pretty well," Mary Jo told her.

Pete pulled into the ranch driveway. "We're almost home. Are they getting warm?"

Mary Jo had her puppy inside her coat. "I think so. At least warmer than they were out in the snow. How could someone be so cruel?"

"I don't know. But these can be our house dogs…if they survive." Pete pressed his lips together.

He dropped Leslie off at her place, then parked the SUV by the back door of the main house. Mary Jo had taken the second puppy from Leslie, and both tiny animals were wriggling as she hurried into the kitchen. Pete took one from her when she almost dropped it.

"Oh, thank you. They're hard to keep hold of."

"Yeah, especially when you have delicate hands," he said. "Why don't you give me the other one, too, while you heat up the milk?"

"Thanks. You saved their lives."

"No, Mary Jo, you did that. It was amazing you even saw them."

"And wonderful that you agreed to take care of them."

"Okay, we'll share the parenting chores for these two. Maybe if they make it, we'll have house pets for our guests. I think that will add to the program."

"Do you, really?" Mary Jo asked, enthusiasm in her voice.

"Yeah, honey, I do," Pete said softly.

After slipping off her coat and washing her hands, Mary Jo opened a can of condensed milk and poured it in a pan to heat. "Okay, let me have one of them," she insisted, petting the shivering puppy and holding it close to her. "I think my hair dryer might be good for them, too. They're still a little wet." She dashed into the back hall to get it.

Pete wasn't sure about that idea, but if it pleased Mary Jo, he wouldn't say no.

Back in the kitchen, she plugged in the hair dryer and turned it on low. "It shouldn't get too hot this way." Spreading several towels on the breakfast table, she put the puppies on them and then gently dried their fur.

The little dogs huddled together, having found each other, and seemed to enjoy the warm air. Just then, Leslie came in with some eyedroppers. "Do you think these will work?"

Mary Jo took them. "Have they been washed?"

"Yes. I don't know why Cliff keeps them, but he carefully cleans them before he puts them away."

"Okay, then let's see if we can get the puppies to eat."

Using the eyedroppers, they tried to feed them. The chocolate-colored one caught on quickly and began to guzzle the milk. The golden puppy seemed less interested, but Mary Jo kept trying and finally it began to swallow.

The smile on her face as she looked up at Pete was the most beautiful sight he'd ever seen.

Chapter Seven

Several times during the night, Mary Jo came to Pete's door to wake him up. Hearing her soft knock, he would crawl out of bed, pull on his jeans and T-shirt, and join her in the kitchen. She always chose to feed the golden puppy. He would feed the chocolate one.

"Pete, I want to thank you," she said at the early morning feeding. "I know it was hard for you to get up, but I really appreciate your help. I couldn't do it without you." She lowered her voice. "Do you think they're going to make it?"

"I think so, Mary Jo, but the vet will have to tell us that." He checked the clock. "We'll go after breakfast."

"Okay. Do you want to eat about eight o'clock?"

That gave him two hours to nap. He wouldn't turn that down. "Yeah, that would be good. Will you knock on my door if I don't get up then? I may go back to sleep."

She gave him an engaging grin. "Me, too. This waking up for feeding is kind of tough, isn't it?"

"Yeah. I don't know how new mothers do it." He smiled back at her. "It wears me out."

"I know. Okay, I'll see you at eight."

As he crawled back into bed, Pete gave thanks for those little puppies. Mary Jo hadn't been so friendly in a long time.

He settled against his pillow, a smile on his lips. Feeling this good was spectacular. He expected to have good dreams this morning.

MARY JO WAS TEMPTED to take the puppies to bed with her. Instead, she waited until they snuggled up together to sleep. She couldn't bear to leave them crying. But once they settled down next to each other, they seemed to feel safe.

Falling into her bed was a relief. Thank

goodness for her lighter schedule. And for Pete's help.

She smiled. It had been a long time since she'd smiled thinking about Pete. But he'd been so good today, so gentle with the puppies, and reassuring when she'd needed it. And he'd performed the difficult task of burying the other puppies. She couldn't have done that so proficiently.

How sad that someone had put those puppies out in the cold, near a stream. That cruelty would stay with her for a long time. But the two surviving puppies were so sweet!

Reminding herself to go to sleep, she closed her eyes, knowing she'd dream of Pete and the puppies.

SOMETHING WAS DISTURBING Pete's sleep. He turned over, but the knocking didn't go away. Slowly, he opened one eye. That's when he remembered he was supposed to get up at eight o'clock. Checking his watch, he threw off the covers and scrambled into his jeans. "I'm coming," he called.

When he opened his door, he found

Mary Jo waiting anxiously at his door. "Sorry, honey, I'll be ready in a moment."

"All right. Breakfast is on the table."

Five minutes later, smooth-shaven, he appeared in the kitchen. "Sorry I was so hard to wake up, Mary Jo. How are the puppies?"

"They're fine. Still sleeping right now." She smiled at him gratefully. "Thanks for getting up so we can go to the vet."

"I didn't really think I'd go back to sleep, but I must've been out like a light."

"Yes. I thought about coming in to wake you up, but I didn't think I should do that."

"It would've been all right," he assured her with a grin.

"Is your breakfast still hot?"

"Yeah, it's great."

Minutes later, they each took a puppy and hurried out to the truck. After Mary Jo climbed in, she reached for his puppy, too.

"You sure you can handle two of them?"

"Of course. I didn't want to make Leslie get up this early."

Pete knew he was going to enjoy the trip more with just the two of them.

"Will the vet be able to tell us what kind of dogs they are?" Mary Jo asked a few minutes later.

"He should be able to. They're obviously some kind of mix. If they were purebreds, their owners wouldn't have abandoned them."

"Oh, you poor babies," she crooned to the puppies. "It's not your fault, is it?"

For the rest of the ride, he smiled, enjoying her soft voice as she spoke to the lucky pups she held against her.

Turning in to the veterinarian's office, he parked and then swiveled around to collect the chocolate-colored puppy. She let that one go, but neither of the puppies was happy being separated.

Once they were in the office, Mary Jo sat down, taking both pups back into her arms. Pete stepped to the receptionist's desk to explain the problem and find out when the doctor could see them.

"He's free now. I'll go tell him you're here."

"Thanks."

She went to the closed door behind her

desk, and came right back out. "He can see you now."

The vet was the one the Ledbetters used at the ranch. As he examined the pups, Mary Jo reached out for Pete's hand.

He didn't think she'd done that since their fight—voluntarily touched him. And he liked it. He squeezed her fingers to comfort her when the puppies cried.

"What did you feed them last night?" the vet asked.

"Canned milk, heated up," Mary Jo replied. "We didn't think they could handle anything else."

"You're right. You'll need to keep them on canned milk at least until their eyes are open, but probably longer. They would still be nursing, so they'll need to grow some before you can stop the milk."

"Okay. Do we need to keep feeding them every four hours?" Pete asked.

"Yeah, just like a baby."

"When do we bring them in for their first shots?" Mary Jo asked.

"Not until they're six weeks old. But if they stop eating, bring them back right away. Are you feeding them with eyedroppers?"

"Yes, it's all we have," Mary Jo said.

"Here are some syringes to use, but be careful and don't choke them."

"Thanks, Doc." Pete shook his hand.

"Just call me if you have problems."

"We will," he promised, and guided Mary Jo out of the office. The puppy he carried, the chocolate one, was whining. When they got in the truck, Pete handed him to Mary Jo. "Do you mind?" he asked. "I think he'll be happier with his brother."

"I know. And I can't stand their pitiful cries."

Pete chuckled. "You're going to be a sucker when your own baby cries, aren't you?"

"I don't know. I haven't even thought about having children."

His voice softened as he added, "I think you'll be a great mother, Mary Jo." As kind and sweet as she was, any kid would be lucky to have her as a mom.

She averted her eyes, looking down at the puppies. "Maybe, if it ever happens."

Pete knew by her body language it was time to change the subject. "I guess it'll be time to feed these little ones again when we get home. Don't you think?"

"Yes, but the feeding should go faster with the syringes."

"I hope so. I'm pretty sure Cocoa will drink faster. I'm not so certain about your puppy," he teased her.

"Cocoa? You've named him?" At Pete's nod, she said, "I did, too. Mine's Goldie. You don't think Goldie's too feminine a name for a boy, do you?"

"Nah. We can say it's short for Golden Boy."

"Oh, good! I've been thinking of him as Goldie. I didn't want to say anything until the vet said they'd be okay."

Pete nodded. "You've probably called him that when you've talked to him, haven't you?"

"Yes," she said softly.

"Well, Goldie he is, then." He reached out and petted the dogs. "Now that they're named, we'll have to get bowls and paint their names on them."

She laughed. "Shouldn't we wait until they start eating solid food?"

Pete laughed in turn. "I guess so."

Mary Jo sobered. "Will your grandfather let us keep them?"

"I believe so. I'll ask him later today."

"If not?"

"Don't worry. I'll talk him into it."

Pete parked the truck in back of the big house and reached out for Cocoa. "Come on, pal. Let's go get some lunch, okay?"

Mary Jo slid out her side of the truck and hurried around it to the back door. Pete pulled out his key and let them in.

"It seems so funny to use a key. During the season, we don't have to," Mary Jo said.

"I know. I never thought I'd say it, but it feels a little lonely now," Pete replied.

"Yes. I think the off periods help us enjoy the guests when they come."

"I agree. And we'll have March and April off next spring."

When they reached the kitchen, Mary Jo passed Goldie to Pete. He sat down at the breakfast table, holding both puppies in his arms while she heated milk and filled the syringes. She handed one to Pete and took Goldie from him. She cuddled the puppy against her chest and began feeding him.

Pete did the same with Cocoa.

After a while he looked at Mary Jo. "How's Goldie doing?"

"After the first minute, he got used to the syringe. He's really doing well now."

"Yeah. Cocoa, too."

As the puppies ate, Leslie came into the kitchen.

They told her about their trip to the veterinarian and how they'd named the puppies.

"So Goldie is a girl?" Leslie asked.

Mary Jo lifted her chin. "No, it's really Golden Boy, but we call him Goldie for short."

"Cute," she said. She hovered over the pups. "Now that they're eating more they might sleep longer."

"Yeah, I hope so!" Pete said, but he was grinning.

"Maybe you can take a nap this afternoon," Mary Jo suggested.

"Only if you—" Pete bit his tongue before he could finish that thought. “I mean, I’m not very good at naps.”

“Well, at least you have another day off before you have to get up and go to work. I’ll try not to wake you this evening.”

“I don’t mind. I want to feed Cocoa.”

“Are you sure?” Mary Jo said.

“Wouldn’t you get up to feed Goldie?” he asked.

“Yes.” Her grin was adorable.

“So wake me up tonight. I’ll be okay.”

“All right.”

Leslie spoke again. “You’ve both done well. But are you going to keep them?”

Pete answered, “Yeah. I think Granddad will agree. We’ll have to do a good job of training them, but I think we’ll manage.”

“I hope so. Did the vet say what kind of dogs they are?”

“He thinks they’re a mix of Lab and something else. If they’d been purebreds, they likely wouldn’t have been abandoned like that.”

“No, I guess not.”

Cliff came into the kitchen then. “Where are these puppies you’ve found?”

Pete nodded toward the box where the pups lay snuggled up to each other, sleeping. "Mary Jo and I want to keep them, Granddad. We'll take care of them, train them."

"You've already got a job, boy. You can't—"

"I can!" Mary Jo exclaimed. "I have a lighter schedule."

"We want your stay to be easier for you, not harder," he argued.

"Please, Cliff? They're so sweet. I'm sure they'll be good-natured dogs!"

Pete caught his grandfather's eye and nodded toward Mary Jo. He tried to convey the thought that the puppies might keep her at the Lazy L. "We'll see how they do," Cliff said, catching on. "They might be something the guests will like."

"Oh, thank you!" she exclaimed.

Once he and Leslie left, Mary Jo threw herself into Pete's arms. "Thank you so much, too!"

He couldn't help but hug her close even as he protested, "Hey, I didn't do anything!"

"Yes, you did. You convinced him to let the puppies stay!"

Pete held her nearer still. "Well, maybe a little bit, but I want them, too."

Suddenly, Mary Jo realized Pete was holding her, and she tried to back out of his embrace. "I'm sorry I—I threw myself in your arms."

"I'm not complaining," he said, even as he released her.

She blushed, but kept moving back. "Um, I guess I should make us some lunch."

"Let's just eat sandwiches. Then we can clean up and play with the puppies until it's time to feed them again."

"Don't we have to let them sleep?"

"Well, yeah, but maybe they'll play a little."

Making sandwiches didn't take long. When they started eating, Pete asked Mary Jo if she'd ever had a dog for a pet. He wasn't surprised to hear she hadn't.

"Did you have any pet?" he pressed.

"Yes, I had a canary. I wanted a dog, but my mother thought one would be too much trouble. She said I'd learn how to take care of a bird. That meant I had to clean the cage once a week. I hated that."

"So what happened to it?"

"Nothing. I cleaned the cage like I was supposed to. But when my brother wanted a puppy, Mother said he had to learn to take care of one, so *he* got the job of cleaning the bird cage, and I didn't have to anymore."

"Did your brother get a puppy?"

"No. After about a year, he let the bird escape. Mother said he wasn't good at taking care of a pet."

Pete chuckled. "I think your mom didn't like animals!"

Mary Jo let out a laugh. "I know. By the time she made my brother take over caring for the bird, I'd realized that."

"Well, you've got your pet now, honey. You've earned the right to have a puppy. And I think Goldie will be the perfect dog for you."

PETE LOOKED FORWARD to his third day off. He'd thought Hank was crazy when he'd suggested altering the schedule, but it was working out well.

Best of all, the puppies had brought him and Mary Jo together. She needed his help, and when they got up to feed the pups during the night, she talked about her home, her brother and her parents, about the puppies growing up, and her ideas for the future.

Pete liked to ask her questions, especially about her life plans. She explained that she already had what she'd dreamed about. "I love cooking for other people, planning meals. It's like a dream come true."

"But what about when you have kids?"

"I—I don't know."

"I would think one day you might get tired of cooking."

"I don't think that'll happen."

It gave him hope that she'd stay at the Lazy L long enough to fall for him again.

After their six o'clock feeding, he set his alarm for quarter to eight. It would surprise Mary Jo that she didn't have to wake him up.

Again he fell asleep deeply, but the alarm woke him and he got up to shower and shave. When she knocked on his door at eight, he opened it at once.

"Oh! You must've set your alarm," she said with a smile.

"Yeah. I didn't want you to have to wake me up. Is breakfast ready?"

"Almost. I'll go finish it."

"I'll come with you. Maybe I can help."

"You could set the table."

"And pour the coffee."

In the kitchen, they worked together, getting breakfast on the table. "Is Hank cleaning up after his breakfast each morning?" Pete asked.

"Mostly. He's left a few things dirty, but he heads out pretty early in the morning."

"You should talk to him about that," Pete suggested.

"No, I don't mind cleaning up a little."

"He's not helpless like the puppies."

"I know he isn't, but he's used to someone helping him out."

Pete laughed. "You're too easy on him, Mary Jo."

"Well, it's my choice."

After breakfast Mary Jo suggested they put the bingo prizes away.

Pete liked the sound of that. At least they'd be together. "Sure, that's a good idea. We certainly can't leave them in the dining room."

"That's what I thought."

"And then it will be time to feed the pups again."

"Yes. They're always hungry, aren't they?"

Pete and Mary Jo smiled at each other.

Their day was full and enjoyable. Pete could feel himself falling deeper and deeper for her. He could only hope she was falling for him.

He helped her make dinner, and put it on the table that evening when his brother came in from work.

After he showered, Hank strolled into the kitchen and plopped down in his chair. "Boy, I'm glad I have the next three days off."

"Will you be able to help with the puppies?" Mary Jo asked him.

"Uh, no, Mary Jo. I'm going into town as soon as I eat."

"I think she meant tomorrow during the day," Pete said.

"Will they take much time?"

"No, they won't," she said.

"What do we have to do with them?"

"Just feed them. We heat up canned milk and pour tiny bits of it in their mouths with syringes. They're very cute."

"Where are they?" Hank asked, looking around the kitchen.

"In that box." She pointed.

He went over and peered into it. "They look kind of scrawny, don't they?"

Pete and Mary Jo both protested.

"Brother, they look better than you did when you were their age!" Pete said.

"Hey, I've seen pictures of me. I was really cute."

"So are they," Mary Jo exclaimed.

"Okay. I guess I can help out, if you think we're going to keep them on the ranch."

"We are!" she said forcefully.

Pete put his arm around her. "If you want

to eat," he told his brother, "I wouldn't argue that fact with our cook here."

Hank looked at the two of them. "Hey, you two stopped bickering?"

Chapter Eight

As if startled by a raging bull, Mary Jo jumped away from Pete. "We…we—"

"Yeah, we have." Pete came to her rescue. "We're friends now."

"Oh. I just wondered," Hank said with a shrug. "Is dinner ready?"

"Coming right up." Mary Jo seemed relieved to busy herself.

Hank sat down in his chair. "Aren't you two going to eat?"

Pete rounded the table and sat down by Mary Jo's place. "Sure we are. We cooked it."

"*You* cooked it? I didn't think you could cook."

"I've learned a lot from Mary Jo." That was an understatement, Pete thought.

Hank just grunted.

"You're going into town tonight?" Pete asked.

"Yeah. I promised the girls I would when I was there Saturday night."

"At least you can sleep late in the morning. But Mary Jo will need your help feeding the puppies at ten."

"But the puppies need to eat at six," Mary Jo reminded him.

"I'll be up at six, Mary Jo, and I want to help while I can."

"All right. I'll wake you up, if you're sure."

"I'm sure."

She smiled at him again, as she had earlier…

Yeah, Pete really loved those puppies!

"PETE, YOU NEED TO COME into town with me tonight," Hank said when Pete returned to the house after work the next day.

"Why?"

"Brenda really has a thing for you. She keeps asking me when you're coming."

Pete flashed a look at Mary Jo, who quickly turned her back on him so he couldn't read her face. He remembered Brenda, the tall blonde with the long legs. But she couldn't compare to the woman in front of him.

"Tell her never."

"Come on, Pete, I can't say that."

"Why not?"

"She won't believe me. She knows you used to come to town all the time."

"Then—"

"Pete, you could go with Hank," Mary Jo interrupted. "I'll get Leslie to help me with the puppies." She kept her head down as she carried a platter to the table.

"No, thanks."

She shot him a confused look.

"I'll feed the puppies with you."

"You want the lady's number?" Hank pressed. "I could get it for you."

"No, thanks." Pete stared at his brother. At times like this he wished they could go out back and fight as they had when they were kids. Maybe then Hank would shut up.

"Pete, I think your grandfather wants

you to—to socialize a little," Mary Jo suggested.

"Why do you say that?" Did she know about Cliff's "plan"?

"He—he's been trying to find someone for you." Mary Jo turned her back again.

"Well, I don't care what he wants. I'm not interested."

And the subject was closed, as far as he was concerned.

There was no conversation during supper. Pete was too angry, and apparently neither Mary Jo nor Hank had anything to say.

After eating quickly, Hank said goodbye to Mary Jo and walked out without speaking to Pete.

"I think your brother is upset with you," she murmured.

"I don't see why he should be. It's no skin off his back if I'm not interested in someone."

"Maybe your grandfather was encouraging him."

"He should know better."

They both heard the puppies start to cry.

"I guess that means they're ready to eat," Pete said, grinning at Mary Jo.

"Yes, I'll put the milk on to warm."

After clearing off the table, Pete picked up both puppies and sat down again.

Mary Jo filled the syringes and brought them over, along with a couple of cloths to mop up any milk the puppies spilled.

"Thanks," Pete said as he took one of the syringes. "Cocoa looks like he's starving."

She settled in the other chair and claimed Goldie. "I put more milk in each syringe, just a little more. I think it might help them sleep longer."

"Good. Look how Cocoa is stretching up to drink."

Mary Jo smiled. "You're making him do that by holding the syringe so high."

"Yeah, I guess I am. But I think he's growing."

"Yes, I believe he is."

When the puppies finished feeding, Pete and Mary Jo carried them back to their box.

"What are you going to do now?" he asked.

She shrugged. "I don't know. Maybe I'll go read a book."

"Why don't we watch another movie? Jessie is going to be unhappy if we've only looked at one of them."

"Are you sure?"

"That Jessie will be irritated? Oh, yeah, I'm sure."

"No, I meant if we should… Never mind. Yes, that sounds fine."

"Okay, I'll go set up the DVD and find those other movies. You make the pop-corn!"

"Popcorn again?"

He put his arm around her and turned her toward the pantry. "Definitely!"

She didn't even resist his kiss. Pete took that as a good sign.

They watched another movie, this one a comedy. Mary Jo sat beside him on the couch. This time he held the popcorn on his lap so she'd sit up against him. And she did.

After the movie they returned to the kitchen and waited for the puppies to wake up.

When they heard a car come down the

driveway, Pete went to the window to investigate. He didn't recognize the vehicle. "I'm going to see who that is. I'll be right back."

"Okay."

A few minutes later, he came into the kitchen with two women about her age. "Mary Jo, we have some visitors."

She stared at the two, both of whom were beautiful. "Hello."

Both greeted her in turn. Then the blonde, whom she'd seen before, explained that they'd been with Hank in town and he happened to mention the puppies.

"We'd just love to see them, Pete, if you don't mind," the woman said.

Pete looked at Mary Jo. She nodded, and he moved to the corner for the box. Carrying it carefully to the table, he showed their visitors the puppies. "They should be waking up in a little bit," he told them. Mary Jo remained by the sink, but her eyes were focused on the box.

"Oh, aren't they sweet," the other woman said.

The blonde wasn't as enthusiastic. "Yes,

just darling. Pete, why didn't you come to town tonight?"

"I didn't want to."

"But I was waiting for you," she said softly.

"I don't believe I made any plans with you, Brenda."

"But I told Hank I wanted to see you." She gave him a sultry look from under her thick lashes.

"Sorry, but I had other things to do."

"I just might have to make some plans with you, so you'll quit being a hermit!"

"No, thanks," Pete said.

"Your grandfather said you needed to get out more," she told him.

"He's wrong."

Mary Jo turned her back at that point, which drew Pete's gaze.

"But, Pete—"

The dogs, probably awakened by the voices, started crying, interrupting Brenda.

"What is that horrible sound?" she whined.

"The puppies. They're waking up."

Pete looked at Mary Jo. "Have you put the milk on?"

"No, I'll do that now."

"You'll have to excuse us. We have to feed them."

"You want me to go?" Brenda asked, a note of shock in her voice.

"Yeah. The puppies take up a lot of time."

"Well, excuse me! I didn't mean to interrupt your nursery work!" She turned and left the kitchen, followed by her friend.

"I'll make sure they leave," Pete said as he walked out of the kitchen.

It was several minutes before he came back.

"Is everything okay?" Mary Jo asked.

"No! Stupid woman."

"What's wrong?" she asked, handing him the syringe for Cocoa.

"That woman thought if she kissed me it would persuade me to come back to town with her!"

"You didn't like it?"

"I didn't let her touch me. I told her no."

"I see."

Pete gave Mary Jo a straight look. "Come feed Goldie," he said.

While they were sitting there with the dogs in their laps, he said, "I think I'm going to need protection."

"Is Cocoa making a mess?"

"Not that kind of protection," he said with a smile. "I mean protection from the women. Apparently, Granddad has enlisted every female he knows to come after me."

"Surely he doesn't know that many."

"Apparently he does know a lot. He's even offered a monetary prize, according to Brenda."

"No! He wouldn't!"

Pete shook his head. "I've got to do something."

"What can you do?"

"I have to find someone to pretend to be my fiancée."

"Maybe she'll convince you to make it real."

"Honey, I can't pretend with any woman from town. It will have to be someone here on the ranch."

He watched her face as what he meant registered. "Pete, you can't mean me!"

"Who else would fit the bill?"

"But...but no, I can't do that."

"Sure you can, honey. I wouldn't ask much of you. You'd just need to hang around."

"Are you sure?"

"You'd be doing me a big favor...as a friend."

Mary Jo let the syringe fall from Goldie's mouth, and the puppy started to wriggle. "Oh. Okay, I'll help you out." She offered the syringe again and he went back to feeding eagerly.

"Thanks, honey. I'll try to make it easy."

Easy? Mary Jo knew it would be anything but.

THEY BOTH GOT UP to feed the puppies in the darkened kitchen. Mary Jo had decided less light might help them get back to sleep.

Pete didn't mind. He enjoyed sitting next to her in the dim room. It was like a romantic candlelit dinner, only the puppies were fed instead of the people.

When the two of them got up at six, however, Mary Jo turned on the overhead light, and after the feeding, started to cook breakfast.

"What are you doing, Mary Jo? I'm supposed to get my own breakfast. Did you forget?"

"No, but you crawled out of bed to feed the puppies. I'm already up, so I'll go ahead and make your breakfast."

"Thanks, sweetheart. That's really thoughtful of you." He watched her for a moment. "Oh, by the way, we need to go into town this evening."

"Why?"

"Because to scare off the other ladies, we need to be seen as a couple. Out in public."

"But tonight? Why don't we wait until tomorrow?"

"Because I want them to start thinking of me as unavailable."

"Do you think that will work?"

"Sure, so don't make any dinner. We'll eat in town."

"WE'RE GOING IN HERE?" Mary Jo asked in surprise as Pete led her into the most popular restaurant in Steamboat Springs.

"Sure. It's where everyone comes."

"But, Pete, don't you think a quieter place would be better?"

"Nope." After a moment, he muttered, "You realize I have to be affectionate, don't you?"

"Yes, I guess so."

"Good. Let's go in."

He slung his arm around her and led her inside. Before the hostess could address them, he leaned down and kissed Mary Jo's lips.

She buried her face in his chest and he held her close. "We need a table for two," he said, grinning.

"I can tell," the hostess said with a knowing smile. "Follow me."

"Come on, honey. I'm starved."

Mary Jo raised her head and stared at him. "All right."

He let her slide into the booth, and then sat beside her. "I think we can both share this bench," he said, draping his arm along the seat back behind her.

"Don't you think we'll be a little

cramped, both of us on the same side of the table?"

"Nope, I think I'd be lonely over there."

They ordered and then he swung around to face her, willing her to participate in his game. He whispered in her ear, enjoying her scent as he got closer. He stroked her cheek, and dared to kiss her several times.

"I think you're overdoing it, Pete," Mary Jo whispered, her voice tense.

"Oh, honey, I don't think they're convinced."

"But, Pete, if you keep on this way, they'll expect to see an engagement ring on my finger. You don't want that, do you?"

"Why didn't I think of it?" he said with enthusiasm.

"What?"

"An engagement ring!"

"No, Pete, definitely not! You don't buy an expensive ring in a situation like this!"

"I think it's a great idea. What kind of ring do you like? Do you want a big diamond?"

"No! I—I don't wear rings. Because of my cooking."

"Really?"

"Really," she said firmly. "Well, sometimes I wear a small ring."

"I'll see what they've got at the jewelry store."

"Pete, I'm serious. I don't think you should do this."

After being interrupted by the arrival of their food, Pete started a conversation about the puppies, which always drew her attention and made her relax.

During dinner, several women stopped by the table to talk to Pete, but he seemed so disinterested they didn't stay long. He always included Mary Jo in the conversation, too, though she didn't have much to say.

He noticed how the women tried to ignore Mary Jo. Her idea was a good one—he couldn't wait to go to the jewelry store for an engagement ring. "What's your ring size?" he asked her.

She gave him a wide-eyed look, then said, "I don't know."

"Liar," he teased. "I bet you do."

"There must be another way!"

"I don't think so. Just in case I have to buy a ring, what size *do* you wear?"

"If you have to, make it simple and small. I wear a size six. But I don't think you should do it."

He leaned over and kissed her lips again. It was so hard to resist her sweetness. "I won't unless I have to, honey, but I think it's a good plan."

"I think your grandfather would be very unhappy that you didn't take this seriously."

"He has no idea how seriously I am taking things, sweetheart."

She fell silent, unwilling to discuss the situation any further.

Pete checked his watch. "You know, the shops are open late on Thursdays. I bet we could find a ring tonight."

"No, I don't think so."

"You want me to miss work tomorrow, to come into town to find a ring?"

"No, I don't want you to do that!"

"Okay, then eat up. We'll stroll down the street to see what we can find."

She wouldn't talk for the rest of the meal.

When they'd finished, he asked, "Would you like coffee?"

"No, thanks. I—I need to go home. The puppies will wake up soon."

"Yeah, I'm sure they'll get up for their bedtime feeding two hours early," he said with a smile, teasing her.

"But—"

He pulled her up from the table. "We'll worry about the babies when it's closer to ten. Don't you think?"

She swallowed. "I just think—"

"I know, honey. But it'll be all right."

He led her outside and down the sidewalk. He was right about the jewelry store being open. Leading her inside, even though she resisted, he asked to see engagement rings. Mary Jo hung back, unwilling to help him make a decision.

Whispering to the salesman, he explained that his fiancée was reluctant to wear a big ring because she was a chef. The jeweler said, "Perhaps you want to put your money into the quality of the ring rather than the size."

"Exactly! That's what I want."

The man pulled out a tray of rings that sparkled brilliantly. When Pete had selected one he liked, he called Mary Jo over. "Do you see anything you fancy?"

"No, I don't."

"That's because you haven't looked at them yet."

He pulled her closer and wrapped his arm around her.

"They're very nice, but…but I don't think—"

He kissed her. "Just pick one."

She whispered, "I don't know how much they cost."

"Just choose the one you like best."

Pete watched her eyes as she looked at the display. He saw them linger over one ring in particular—the one he'd picked out himself. When she refused to decide, he selected that one.

"What size is it?" he asked.

"A size six," the salesman said.

"Honey, it was made for you. Let's try it on."

Chapter Nine

Mary Jo stared at the ring on the third finger of her left hand. She couldn't seem to stop looking at it. But she knew she should take it off. It didn't really mean anything.

It couldn't.

So why was she still wearing it?

Because it represented a dream, a dream that couldn't come true.

Pete came into the kitchen and caught her staring at the ring. "Do you like it?"

"I think it must've been very expensive!"

"It's well worth it. Think of the peace you'll give me. I won't have all those women hitting on me."

"I agree with your grandfather. You *do* need to find a woman."

"What are you?"

"I beg your pardon?" she asked, irritated with him.

"Honey, you are a lady, a beautiful lady. With you at my side, I don't have to worry about those other gals. And you're a lot classier."

"But I'm not going to sleep with you, Pete. Some of those women are willing to do that!"

"I know you're not, honey. I remember. But I'm going for quality this time, not a cheap date."

"I don't think I understand, but just let me know when you want this ring back. I'll be careful not to lose it."

"Good."

Leslie and Cliff came into the kitchen just then, surprising them. Mary Jo immediately hid her hand.

"Hi, we came by earlier, but no one was here," Cliff said.

"We went to town for dinner…and a little shopping," Pete explained.

"Oh, what did you buy?" Leslie asked.

"Show them, honey," he suggested. "We don't want to hide things from them."

Mary Jo gave him a distressed look, but he put his arm around her and raised her left hand. She blushed when Leslie screamed and grabbed her wrist.

"Oh, that's so wonderful! When is the wedding?"

Cliff frowned. "I don't understand."

"It's not complicated, Granddad. Mary Jo and I are going to get married."

"I think that's lovely, Mary Jo. Did he surprise you?" Leslie asked excitedly.

She looked at Pete. "Kind of."

"Wait until Jessica hears this!" the other woman said, still beaming. "We won't have a shower until they're back."

"Yes, I think we'd better wait on that," Mary Jo said, looking frantically at Pete. "Don't you think?"

"Whatever you want, honey."

Mary Jo rolled her eyes when Leslie and Cliff turned to talk to him. "Yes, we'll definitely wait."

"So you haven't decided on a date?" Leslie asked.

"We will as soon as Mary Jo is ready. I don't want to push her."

"Pete!" she protested.

"What's the holdup?" Cliff asked. "He's bought you a ring. You could take your honeymoon in November when we do."

"I think she wants to see if I'm a one-woman man. I can understand her problem. But I'm a patient guy."

Mary Jo had had enough. She couldn't take one more minute of this talk. The pretense was already burning a hole straight through her heart. "Would anyone like some cookies? I baked a new kind today. And I have a pot of decaf on."

Cookies always got to Cliff. "That sounds good to me. Leslie, you want a snack?"

"I'd love one. Thanks, Mary Jo. We really do miss your cooking for us."

"I know. We didn't do lunch this week. The puppies kept me busy."

"How are they? Goldie and Cocoa, right? I think those names are perfect."

"Yes, we like them, too. I hope they grow up soon. These feedings every four hours are difficult."

"It's the way it will be when you have

a baby," Leslie said with a chuckle. "And they don't grow up as fast, I can tell you."

"Yes, I guess you're right."

Mary Jo must not have looked enthusiastic, for Cliff asked, "You do want children, don't you?"

"Oh, yes, I do," she said with enough conviction to satisfy him. "When…when the time is right."

Pete took her in his arms. "Don't worry, Granddad. I intend to have a talk with my fiancée about things like that."

"Good. I think you should have a child right away. We need to start the next generation."

"I don't know," he said, turning his eyes to Mary Jo. "It would need to be between guest sessions. Maybe this time next year."

Pregnant by Christmas? Mary Jo felt herself stiffen like a frozen turkey. She didn't move even when Pete pulled her closer to him and kissed her.

Only when he leaned in for another toe-curling, all-too-real kiss did she sidestep and escape. She poured the coffee and put a plate of cookies on the table. The calories she planned to consume would be worth it if eating kept her from having to talk. Or, worse yet, kiss Pete.

He sat down beside her and took a cookie. Maybe he wanted to avoid more talk, too.

"You know, Granddad, I want you to know that I'm in favor of the way things have gone here at the ranch," he stated. "I'll admit it took me awhile to think of this place as more than just a cattle operation, but now I'm ready to support Jim and help him turn this into a first-class dude ranch. With Mary Jo's cooking, we're sure to be a hit with the tourists."

"That's true. We got a lot of comments about the food, especially the desserts." Cliff smiled at her.

"I think I've gained a few pounds since I began eating here, too," Leslie said.

"You look beautiful, Leslie," Mary Jo said.

"I agree," Cliff declared.

Suddenly, they heard a whimpering sound.

"Sounds like it's feeding time," Pete

said. “Can you warm up the milk, honey, while I fetch the puppies?”

Mary Jo got up to prepare the milk and fill the syringes.

“I’m not sure keeping these pups is a good idea,” Cliff complained. “They seem to be a lot of trouble.”

“Too late, Granddad. We’re attached to them.”

“Please, can we keep them?” Mary Jo asked, not noticing the look Pete gave his grandfather.

“Oh, well, I guess it’s okay if you’re willing to feed them.”

“I think the guests will appreciate having dogs to play with on a dude ranch. The kids will love them,” Pete pointed out.

“You’re probably right.”

“Thank you, Cliff.” Mary Jo smiled at him.

Leslie took her husband’s hand and said, “I think it’s time we went home. We’re very happy for you. And we’ll plan on lunch next week, okay, Mary Jo?”

“Yes, let’s, Leslie.”

Pete was holding the puppies and was

trying to soothe them. But they wanted their milk, and kept squirming. Mary Jo handed one syringe to him, then reached for Goldie, getting some milk into his mouth.

"Good night. Glad you came by," Pete said as their guests were leaving.

He and Mary Jo were quiet while the puppies suckled. After their tummies were full, Mary Jo took both of them back to their towel-lined box.

When she returned to the table, she said, "I think we need to talk about this pretend engagement."

"I think it's working just fine. Granddad won't be sending any females in my direction anymore. He can concentrate on Hank."

"I don't think that's fair. Does your brother have a clue what's coming?"

"I don't know. He can weather the storm, though."

"But you couldn't? I don't understand how you've survived this long if your grandfather was trying to marry you off."

"He just got in the marrying mood recently, with both he and Jessie getting married."

"How long do we have to pretend?"

"Not too long."

"But—"

"It's not that hard, is it? You're not looking around for another guy, are you?" He slid his arms around her and gave her a peck on the cheek.

"Why did you do that?"

"I just wanted to thank you for helping me…and to say good night."

"You're going to bed?"

"Yes, but wake me up for the next feeding."

"All right, if you're sure."

"I'm sure. Just look at your finger."

"My finger?"

She glanced down, and in the overhead light, the diamond winked.

PETE WAS GLAD he was working today and tomorrow. It was better not to spend too much time around Mary Jo. He might lose his head and forget the role he was playing.

A lot depended on his grandfather's reaction. If he believed their performance last night, he would likely start working on Hank. Pete couldn't repress a grin.

Maybe Hank would hold his grandfather's attention, and Pete could concentrate on Mary Jo. Smiling, he thought about his pretend fiancée. She'd looked so cute last night, her cheeks turning red and her eyes wide as he kissed her.

He'd like to tell her the truth—that he truly loved her. He'd loved her when she'd slept with him the first time, but he hadn't realized it. Only when he'd betrayed her and lost her had he realized what he'd done.

But he was afraid to tell her the truth.

He might scare her away.

Sighing, he turned his horse to follow the fence line. It was a good thing they weren't herding today. He might've missed a cow or two, lost in thoughts of Mary Jo. And the cowboys would've teased him unmercifully.

By the end of the day, he felt sure Mary Jo would welcome him home. Should he take her to town tonight? He'd rather stay in, just the two of them.

Pete guessed he'd have to play it by ear, see what she wanted to do.

Eagerly, he hurried to the house. He could almost feel Mary Jo's arms around his neck, taste her lips on his.... Heading straight to the kitchen, he discovered it empty.

He whirled around and went to Mary Jo's room. Knocking, he waited for her to open the door. She didn't.

Going back to the kitchen, he found the puppies in their box, sound asleep. Pete went through to the dining room and called her name.

No answer.

Where could she be? The puppies were due to wake up shortly. He didn't think she would abandon them, even if she wasn't there for him.

How silly to be jealous of innocent dogs.

Suddenly, he heard a noise coming from overhead. He called again, "Mary Jo?"

"Yes?"

He started up the stairs. "What are you doing up there?"

She appeared at the top of the steps. "Sorry, I didn't know you'd come in."

"But why are you upstairs?"

"Jessica and Jim called. They're coming back tomorrow. And they've decided to take over the front bedroom upstairs."

"And they asked you to do some work for them?"

"No, I just thought since I had some time, I might check out the room and make sure it's in good shape."

"Why are they coming back so early?"

"They said they were homesick," she explained.

Pete frowned. "When do they get in?"

"At ten-thirty, apparently. I told them Hank would pick them up. He wasn't too happy about it, but it's his day off."

"I hope nothing's gone wrong for them."

"I hope not, too. What...what are we going to tell them?"

"About what?" Pete asked blankly.

"This!" she said, holding out her left hand. "This pretense!"

"We're going to continue it! We have to, until things die down."

"But Jessica is my friend. I can't… It's not the same."

"Honey, I know it will be hard, but you can do it. Just relax and tell her we're in love."

"She won't believe me."

"She will if you sound sincere. Besides, she's still on her honeymoon. She'll believe everyone is in love."

Mary Jo stared at him. "Okay, I'll try."

"Thanks, sweetheart." He bent and kissed her. "I know you can do it."

She gave him a troubled look. Then she slipped past him down the stairs to the kitchen.

He followed. "Did you tell Granddad about Jessica?"

"No. I thought you or Hank should tell him."

"Did Hank?"

"No. He was too anxious to get to town."

"So we'll be having dinner alone tonight?"

"No. I asked Leslie and Cliff to come over."

"Can I do anything to help you get dinner ready?"

"No. It's in the oven. They won't be here until seven."

"I have to wait until seven to eat? I'm starving!"

"I thought you would be." She walked to the fridge and took out a bowl filled with cake and ice cream.

"Dessert before dinner? Thanks, honey!" he said, pulling out a chair and sitting down. He dug in, then paused to thank her again.

Just as he finished his treat, the puppies began stirring. Mary Jo hurriedly began filling syringes with warm milk. "I'm not going to be able to feed them right now. Can you cope with both puppies?"

"Sure, somehow. I'll get them." He picked up the crying pups and held them both against his chest. "Listen, guys, you have to be patient. We're feeding you as fast as we can."

The puppies squirmed, so he cradled one in each arm and held them tight. Mary Jo handed him one syringe and then the other, and by crossing his wrists he could feed both puppies at once.

"Hey, this actually works," he declared. "But it's a good thing they don't have to be burped."

Mary Jo laughed.

As the puppies ate, Pete relaxed, watching her prepare some side dishes at the counter. When he heard the older couple entering, he called a welcome.

"What are you doing, boy?" Cliff asked.

"I'm feeding both puppies—two at once. Leslie, do you want to take one?"

"Of course I do." She bent and picked up Goldie.

"Hmm," Pete said. "I'm not sure why women always go for the yellow pup."

"Because he's so sweet," Leslie said with a grin.

"I think Cocoa is just as sweet. But he's my puppy, so I guess I'm prejudiced. Goldie belongs to Mary Jo."

Cliff sat down at the table across from him. "By the way, Granddad," Pete added, "I have some news for you. It seems Jessie and Jim are coming in tomorrow. Hank is picking them up in Denver at ten-thirty."

"What? Why? Is something wrong?"

"You'll have to ask Mary Jo. She didn't seem to think they sounded upset."

Cliff turned to her. "Did Jessie seem odd when you talked to her, Mary Jo?"

"No, Cliff, she didn't. She said they were homesick. I checked on the room they want to use, the front bedroom upstairs. It's ready for them."

"Did they decide that before they left?" he asked.

"No, but she said they'd been thinking about it and figured it would be more practical to take that room for their own instead of remodeling any rooms behind the kitchen."

"Hmm, that's probably true. But we'll have fewer guest rooms available."

"I don't think that's a problem," Mary Jo said.

"I'll have to sit down and figure it out," Cliff murmured, wandering out of the kitchen, looking for paper and pen.

"I hope he doesn't get lost. He can spend hours on the financing."

"Are we doing okay for money?" Pete asked.

"We sure are. In fact, this past summer was more successful than he'd ever thought it would be."

"Glad to hear it. If we were going broke, Mary Jo might leave me!"

"Pete Ledbetter, how dare you say such a thing!" Mary Jo retorted, a note of anger in her voice.

Chapter Ten

The dining room table looked beautiful. The white linen tablecloth and six china place settings would give Jessica and Jim's welcome-home lunch the celebratory air it deserved.

Mary Jo wanted them both to know that they'd been missed. And she wanted to pretend that nothing had happened while they were gone.

She wanted so badly to pull off her ring, but she couldn't. It would be a betrayal of Pete, and she couldn't bring herself to do that.

She checked her watch. It was almost time for their arrival. Hearing the back door opening, she went into the kitchen and discovered Cliff and Leslie taking off their coats.

"Any sign of them?" he asked.

"No, Cliff. I told Hank to call when they started back, but I guess he forgot."

"Humph! That's just like him. *I'll* call," the old man grumbled, pulling out his cell phone.

"Boy, why didn't you call Mary Jo like you said you would?" he said a minute later.

Both Mary Jo and Leslie waited expectantly.

"Well, hurry up, okay?" Cliff barked. "Lunch is ready." He disconnected the phone and looked at them. "He forgot, of course. They're about fifteen minutes away."

"Good. I think everything will be ready just when they get here," Mary Jo said.

"Where's Pete?" Cliff asked next.

"He's working today. He won't be here for lunch."

The rancher pulled his phone back out and dialed another number. "Pete, why aren't you coming to lunch…? Well, never mind that. Get in here…." He paused, then said, “Yeah, I’ll tell her.” He turned around and said, “Pete’ll be here. He’s riding in.”

“I’ll add another plate.”

“I’ll do it, Mary Jo.” Leslie opened the silverware drawer, then headed for the dining room.

“Put him on the end, Leslie,” Mary Jo said. She knew it was right that he be there for his sister’s return, but she also knew he’d call attention as soon as he could to the ring she wore. For some reason, he seemed very proud of their…pretense. That was the only word she could use to describe what this ring represented.

Ten minutes later, she heard Pete come in. He stuck his head in the kitchen. “Have they arrived?”

“Not yet. You have time for a quick shower.”

“Thanks, sweetheart,” he called, and blew her a kiss.

“That boy has really changed, hasn’t he?” Cliff said, staring at the door when Pete had stood.

She said nothing.

"Don't you think, Mary Jo?" the older man pressed.

"Yes, he has."

"I didn't believe it at first. But he's real attached to you."

Leslie came in just then. "What are you talking about?"

"How much Pete has changed."

"He sure has, and I suspect Mary Jo has a lot to do with that."

"Oh, no, I—I didn't do anything."

She was saved by the sound of a truck in the driveway. She looked out the window and cried, "They're here!"

She, Leslie and Cliff were all at the front door by the time the truck came to a halt. Jessica and Jim got out and hugged each of them in turn. Jim asked about Pete, and Mary Jo said he would be along shortly.

Hank began taking suitcases out of the truck, and Jim turned and helped him. Cliff offered a hand, but Jim told him they had it under control.

Mary Jo assured them she'd made certain their bedroom had clean linens and was all ready for them. Jim thanked her and followed Hank up the stairs. Then Jessica said they'd brought an extra bag home with them. "It has gifts for everyone!"

Leslie beamed at her. "This is as exciting as Christmas!"

Jessica was holding Mary Jo's hand. "We had to bring rewards for everyone who stayed here to work. Especially Mary Jo!"

She pulled her hand free. "I need to get the food on the table. If you'll excuse me."

As soon as she'd slipped away, Jessica looked at Leslie. "Is everything all right?"

"Oh, yes, it's better than all right. But I don't want to spoil the surprise."

"What—" Jessica began, but her husband and Hank came down the stairs and interrupted.

"I can't wait for one of Mary Jo's meals," Jim declared.

Mary Jo called them all to the table just then.

They all filed into the dining room, where Mary Jo was arranging serving dishes filled with food. She'd just set a casserole on the table when Pete appeared in the doorway. He greeted his sister and brother-in-law, then took the seat at the head of the table, next to Mary Jo.

During lunch Mary Jo concentrated on eating. She didn't want anyone to notice her ring. In fact, though she hadn't removed it, she'd turned the diamonds inward so only the metal band was visible.

Pete, of course, noticed it almost right away.

"What happened to your ring?" he asked.

"Nothing, Pete. It's—it's just turned around."

"Jess, did you notice Mary Jo's ring?" he asked his sister.

"What ring?"

"Twist it back, honey, so Jess can see it."

"Not now," Mary Jo whispered.

"Yes, now."

She readjusted the diamonds, and Pete grabbed her hand to show Jessica.

"Who gave you that?" his sister squealed.

Pete waited for Mary Jo to reply. Finally, he said, "I did. We're engaged."

In the stunned silence, Cliff said, "It's been good for the boy. He's going to settle down like he should."

"That's wonderful!" Jessica exclaimed, beaming at her friend.

"Good for you," Jim said. "I can recommend married life."

"When's the wedding?" Jessica asked next.

"She hasn't agreed to a date yet," Pete told them.

"I think they should go ahead and go on their honeymoon right away, since you'll be here to cook for Hank and Jim," Cliff said to his granddaughter.

"I thought of something else that has changed," Mary Jo said, trying to change the subject. "We found some puppies, two of them, and we're keeping them. They're in the kitchen."

"Where did you get them?" Jim asked.

Pete shook his head. "They were abandoned along the road when they were so small their eyes were still shut. Three of them were drowned in Butcher Creek. Mary Jo spotted two on the stream bank. We saved them and brought them to the ranch."

"Pete...Pete got the other three and buried them." Mary Jo was reminded again of how thoughtful he'd been. "We've been feeding those two with syringes the vet gave us. You should see them gulp down their warm milk."

"Can I see them now?" Jessica asked.

"Sure, come on, I'll show you." Mary Jo got up and led her away, but her best friend turned to her as soon as they entered the kitchen.

"Tell me about the engagement!"

"Aren't they cute?" Mary Jo asked as she leaned over the box, ignoring Jessica's remark. Then she turned her back, taking the dessert she'd made out of the fridge. It was a carrot cake, with a sinful cream cheese icing. "Do you think everyone will want a piece of this?"

"Of course they will. But you haven't answered my question."

"No, I haven't. Can you take in the plates?"

"Mary Jo! Why aren't you telling me about your engagement?"

"Because I don't know what to say."

"Do you love my brother?"

"You know I do."

"All right. I'll take the plates in, but we'll talk later."

"Okay."

What had she agreed to? Mary Jo couldn't lie to her best friend.... But she'd promised Pete she'd act as if the engagement was real. She was so confused.

Back in the dining room she concentrated on serving and then eating dessert, instead of talking. Pete leaned over and kissed her to say thank-you, and she felt her cheeks turning hot. "Pete!" she whispered in protest.

He leaned forward again to whisper, "It's all right. We're engaged, remember?"

Getting up to clear the table, she soon made her escape into the kitchen. Jessica and Leslie brought in the rest of the plates.

"Oh, thanks. I'll do the dishes. I know you have things to do, Leslie, and Jessica, you need to unpack."

"Don't be silly, Mary Jo. We're not going to dump all this work on you," her friend declared.

"I don't have anything I need to do,

Mary Jo. I don't mind cleaning up." Leslie began scraping plates and handing them to Mary Jo to rinse.

With three of them, it took almost no time to clean the kitchen. It was what would come next that Mary Jo dreaded.

"Okay, now tell me about the engagement," Jessica said.

Mary Jo glanced at Leslie. "It just happened," she finally confessed. "Pete and I were having dinner in town and—and he wanted to..."

"Wait! You and Pete were having dinner in town?" Jessica asked. "Why?"

"Pete thought it would be fun. Hank was already out for the evening and—and Pete thought we should go, too."

Jessica looked at Leslie. "Were you with them?"

"No. We all had lunch in town on Sunday after church, but we weren't with them that evening. We found them here getting ready to feed the puppies later, and they showed us the ring then. It's beautiful, isn't it?"

"Yes. I didn't think Pete would know

how to do that. I mean, I guess you picked out the ring, didn't you?"

"No, I—I was worried about the cost, but Pete…he chose it." Mary Jo was being as honest as she could in the circumstances.

"So how did he ask you?"

"He started talking about getting me a ring while we were at dinner. I didn't think he was serious at first. But after we ate, he took me to the jewelry store in town."

"You are happy, aren't you, Mary Jo?"

"Yes, Jessica, I'm happy."

Fortunately, the puppies woke and started to whine. Mary Jo asked Jessica if she'd like to feed one.

"Oh, that will be fun. Leslie, would you like to take the other one?"

"I would. I was there when Mary Jo found the puppies. Which one do you want to feed—Cocoa or Goldie?"

"Either one." Jessica went to the box and gently picked up Goldie, then handed him over. She sat down with Cocoa and stroked his soft fur. "When will their eyes open?"

"I don't know," Mary Jo said. "We've

had them a couple of weeks. I think it should be soon."

"They're so sweet, but I can't make mine stop crying," her friend complained.

"Nothing will satisfy them until they get their milk," she said with a laugh.

"How often do they eat?" Jessica asked.

"Every four hours."

"Do you have to get up with them at night?"

"Yes, I'm afraid so. But they don't take long to feed." Mary Jo filled the syringes and handed them to Leslie and Jessica.

The women cooed over the puppies and petted them as they ate.

Mary Jo leaned against the kitchen cabinet. She loved having Jessica back, as long as she didn't have to answer any awkward questions.

When the puppies' tummies were full, Mary Jo put both animals back in the box.

Just then all four men came into the kitchen.

"Where are the dogs?" Jim asked.

Like a proud mama, Mary Jo showed him the sleeping puppies.

Pete slipped his arm around her. "Mary Jo's doing a good job of taking care of them, just like they're real babies."

Jim smiled at his wife. "Well, we've got some unpacking to do. We'll bring your gifts down at dinnertime."

"I'll be gone to town by then," Hank said, "but I'll see you tomorrow." He looked as if he was ready to head out any minute.

Jim laughed. "I guess you like these winter hours."

"Yeah, it's worked out for both of us, right, Pete?"

He nodded. "It's like we're on vacation, too."

"Well, that will give you a chance to rest up for the winter session." Jim studied Hank's face.

"Leslie and Pete and I bought a lot more prizes for the bingo nights," Mary Jo interjected.

"And Mary Jo and I checked out a couple of the movies," Pete added.

"How wonderful!" Jessica gave Mary Jo a curious look.

"Yeah, one was a go and one wasn't."

Pete grinned at his sister. "Actually, I liked the one that was a no, but she overruled me."

Jessica laughed. "I think I might trust her judgment over yours, Pete."

"Yeah, I figured," he retorted cheerfully.

"Come on, Jess. I want to get unpacked," Jim said, pulling her toward the stairs.

"All right, I'll see everyone tonight, except for Hank. And Mary Jo, I'll come down and help with dinner. Granddad, will you and Leslie be here?"

"Yeah, I think we will. Is that okay with you, Leslie?"

"Sure, Cliff, that will be fine. And I'll come help with the kitchen chores, too."

"It sounds like I'll have a lot of help," Mary Jo said with a wide smile.

"I've got to go back out until dinnertime," Pete announced, hoping everyone would disappear.

Cliff looked at him. "Well, what are you waiting for?"

"I thought it would be nice to have a minute with Mary Jo," he answered testily.

"Oh! Yes, of course," Leslie said, tugging on her husband's arm. "Come on, Cliff. Let's give them some privacy."

Jim led Jessica toward the stairs, a grin on his face, too.

Soon the kitchen was empty except for Pete and Mary Jo.

She immediately turned her back to him. But that didn't stop him from putting his arms around her.

"What's wrong? Are you embarrassed?"

"Yes!"

He turned her to face him, and after kissing her, said, "I think it's only fair that I get a couple of minutes with you. I won't see you until five o'clock."

"Why are you coming in that early?"

"It's getting dark earlier, and horses don't have lights on them."

"I guess that's true. I didn't think of that."

"Besides, we'll have more time together. And that's a good thing, isn't it?"

"Pete, don't you think I should tell Jessica—"

"No, I don't." He kissed her again, more deeply this time.

"B-but—"

"You're wearing my ring, sweetheart. That's the truth, and I don't think you should have to explain anything to Jessie."

"But she thinks—"

"Yeah, and she's right." He kissed her again, something he really liked doing, before telling her goodbye and escaping out the back door.

Mary Jo slowly sank down into one of the chairs at the table, confused and worried. She was wearing his ring, that was true. But they were pretending. Sometimes she forgot that fact.

That's what made this fake engagement hard. She *wanted* it to be real.

AFTER DINNER THAT EVENING, Jim asked Pete to shoot some pool. He reluctantly agreed, but sent Mary Jo a look that everyone could read.

"We can play while the ladies are cleaning up," Jim said.

"Man, my sister didn't train you right. I usually help Mary Jo with the dishes."

"Yeah, but she's got Jess and Leslie to help tonight."

After stealing a kiss from an embarrassed Mary Jo, Pete followed him to the pool table at one end of the living room.

Jim broke, and the two men watched the balls roll into position on the table.

"How did you convince Mary Jo to get engaged?" he inquired.

"I asked her. How do you think?"

"Don't get me wrong. We're happy about it. But when we left, you weren't speaking to her."

"She wasn't speaking to me is a more accurate statement."

"Okay, that's true. So how did you change her mind?"

"I asked her if we couldn't at least be friends. I got her to go for a horseback ride with me and Hank. I apologized again. Then we ran into a freak snowstorm. We both took care of her and got her back to the house about nine-thirty that night. She thawed toward me a little after that."

"That's still a long way from being engaged."

"That's where the puppies came in. She and Leslie and I went into Steamboat Springs, and on the way home, she spotted them. We've spent a lot of time together feeding them."

"Hank doesn't help?"

"No. He's wrapped up in the nightlife of Steamboat Springs."

"That's not good."

"I know, but I went through that stage a few years back. I think he'll survive."

"You realize you've made a promise to Mary Jo, don't you?"

"Yeah. One I'm prepared to keep. Eager to keep. She may not be sure of that yet, but I didn't want anyone else to come sniffing around."

Jim smiled. "I'm glad we had this talk. Now I can reassure my wife. She's a little protective of Mary Jo."

"I am, too. We'll get married as soon as she's ready. Tell Jessie to be patient."

"Right. I'm not sure it will work, but I'll try."

Chapter Eleven

After Jim had a talk with his wife, Jessica did feel easier about the situation. But not much.

She found that most of the time Pete was around, Mary Jo wasn't completely at ease with him. Jessica didn't know why. But she could admit that their mutual caring for the puppies seemed sincere.

When she got up the next morning, Mary Jo was all excited about the puppies having opened their eyes during the night.

"When will they wake up again?" Jessica asked, curious to see for herself.

"I don't know exactly. I'm giving them more milk, but we want to break them of the late-night feedings."

"Did Pete get up with you for that?"

"Oh, yes. He insists, even though I know he's not getting much sleep."

"That's kind of unusual for him, isn't it?"

Mary Jo glared at her friend. "Pete has been wonderful. He's taken me out to eat and helped with chores when he didn't have to. I don't have anything to complain about."

"I'm glad. I was just wondering...I mean, when I left, you weren't speaking to him."

"You were gone almost three weeks, Jessica. There were just the three of us here, and Hank went to town a lot of the time. Pete and I—we spent some time together."

"I'm glad you watched a couple of the movies," Jessica hurriedly said, hoping to change the subject.

"Yes, Pete insisted. Of course, he insisted on popcorn each time, too."

"I'm sure he did. He loves to eat."

"He does," Mary Jo murmured, then couldn't think of anything else to say.

"So, have you thought about when you're going to get married?"

"No, not yet."

"Well, I can take over the cooking whenever you're ready for a break."

"But I promised to cook until November. You came back early, but that doesn't mean you need to start work early."

"Are you sure?"

Mary Jo nodded. "The guys are cooking their own breakfast now. I don't start work until eight o'clock."

"Who suggested that?"

"Pete. He told Hank he had to make his own breakfast and clean up after himself."

"Pete? Pete said that?"

Mary Jo smiled at her friend. "He's changed a little, hasn't he?"

"Yes, I guess he has."

"I think Leslie's excited about their trip. She said they're going to visit her sons in Denver and Kansas City, to introduce Cliff to them."

"We offered to let them leave at once, but they couldn't change their tickets. I hope Granddad likes her boys…and they like him."

"Me, too. But they're sure to be nice. I

can't imagine Leslie having ill-mannered children."

Jessica shook her head. "I can't, either, but you never know. Raising kids is tricky."

"That's true."

The puppies woke up and Mary Jo put some milk on to warm. "You want to get them and I'll prepare their meal?"

"Okay. How are you, puppies? Can I pick you up?" she asked, doing so tenderly.

It wasn't long before Mary Jo had the milk ready. She handed one syringe to Jessica and kept one, picking up Goldie from the kitchen table.

"I guess we shouldn't let them walk on the table. It's a bad habit," Jessica stated.

"I think the puppies will eat from a dish, once they get beyond the milk-only stage."

"When will that be?"

"I'm not sure. I guess we'll have to ask the vet."

"I'm glad you took the puppies to the vet right away," Jessica said.

"Yes, we were afraid they'd die. Seeing the other three down in the water was heartbreaking."

Jessica nodded. "It was good of Pete to bury them."

"I was afraid to ask him because I knew it would be a grisly job. But he took care of it."

"Is he working today?"

"Yes. It's Saturday, one of Hank's days off."

"Jim said he might—" Jessica was cut off as her husband came in, as if on cue.

"I might what?" he asked after he kissed her.

"I was about to tell Mary Jo that you might offer to work Wednesdays and Thursdays. That way Hank and Pete would only have to work two days a week."

"That would be nice of you, Jim," Mary Jo said. "I didn't know you could handle cows."

Jessica didn't like to brag, but it was obvious she was proud of her husband. "Before he worked on Wall Street he used to be the ranch manager on his dad's spread. But his parents wanted him to go to college."

"I didn't know that."

Jim nodded. "I'd feel like a slacker not

working at all." He looked up at the clock. "Hey, when is lunch?"

Jessica chastised him, but Mary Jo grinned. "We're eating at twelve-thirty. Can you hold out that long?"

He nodded sheepishly. "I guess I'll go do some more paperwork."

Jessica waited until he left the room, then, with a big sigh, said, "I love him so much!"

Mary Jo sighed in turn. "I know what you mean."

On Monday, Pete wanted to do something with Mary Jo. But she was determined to bake sugar cookies and decorate them for Halloween.

"What do you do to them? Are you going to make orange icing?" he asked.

"Yes. And I've got some cookie cutters in the shape of a pumpkin, a witch's hat, and other things."

"Okay. I can help with that."

"Pete, you're being really sweet, but you don't have to do this."

"I want to do something with you, and I'll enjoy it."

"All right. If you're sure."

"I'm sure." He gave her a wide grin. "As long as I get to sample a few cookies."

He stood beside her as she mixed up the dough, handing her the ingredients she asked for. Then she rolled it out and together they used the cookie cutters to make three dozen cookies.

After she put them in the oven, she began making the frosting.

"This looks like chocolate," Pete said, staring in a pan.

"It is. It's dark chocolate."

"I think I like it. What do we use it for?"

"The witch's hat, the inside of the pumpkin, the black cat. It will have lots of uses."

"And the orange? How'd you make that?"

"With powdered sugar and food coloring."

"When do we start decorating?"

She smiled at him. "After the cookies cool."

"I can see our kids asking the same thing, can't you?"

The smile faded from her face and she pulled away. "No, I don't think so."

"I do. We're going to marry, Mary Jo. And we're going to have children who love their mommy's cookies."

"You're acting as if this engagement is real. You know better, Pete. You said we would just pretend for a little while."

"I changed my mind, sweetheart. I love you."

She backed away. "Don't—don't say that!"

He held up his hands and stepped back, too. "Okay, we'll just take it a day at a time, Mary Jo. Come on, let's decorate some cookies, okay?"

She gave him a doubtful look. "I guess so."

He settled down at the table, afraid to open his mouth for fear he'd scare her off again. Quietly, he waited for the cookies to cool after they came out of the oven.

Jessica entered the kitchen awhile later to discover her brother decorating cookies. "Want some help?"

"Sure. I think Mary Jo baked enough for an entire school of kids. You can do the chocolate."

"Chocolate? Now I know I want to help!"

Mary Jo joined them, but Pete noticed she chose Jessica's side of the table when she sat down.

An hour later, Pete leaned back. "Can I have my sample now?"

"Of course you can," Mary Jo said. "You've done a good job. Your pumpkins are the best!"

"Thanks, honey. Your witches are better than mine, though."

"Yeah, as long as you don't say *she* looks like a witch," Jessica said with a grin.

"I'd never say that. She looks more like an angel to me."

Jessica stared at her brother. "You really mean that, don't you?"

"Yeah, I do."

Mary Jo's cheeks turned rosy and she didn't say anything.

"I didn't believe your engagement was for real at first, but I'm beginning to think you two are in love."

Pete stared at Mary Jo. "Oh, yeah, we are." He watched as she peeped up at him and then turned away. He wasn't sure he'd ever be able to convince her that he truly loved her.

She avoided getting close to him. They still took care of the puppies, of course, but the pups were growing quickly. Soon they'd be eating puppy food, and much more independent.

This afternoon, with Jessica there, Mary Jo couldn't run away. But Pete's efforts to convince her that their engagement was real to him were having no effect, other than to have her backing away.

He decided he should take Jessica aside and tell her the truth. She might be able to help him convince Mary Jo he was sincere.

When they finished decorating the cookies, he followed Jessica as she left the kitchen.

"Jessie? Do you have a minute to chat?"

His sister turned and stared at him. "You want to chat?"

"Yeah. Maybe in the living room?"

"Why?"

He looked around. "I don't want Mary Jo to hear us."

With a frown, Jessica motioned for him to follow her. Once they were in the living room, she led the way to the sofa farthest from the kitchen. "Pete, I swear, if you break her heart again, I'll never forgive you!"

"No! That's just it! I need to explain that—that she thinks I'm pretending because a lot of the women in Steamboat Springs were coming on to me. And they were. But I love Mary Jo. I've been faithful to her ever since I—I broke my leg."

"You mean you're sleeping with her?" His sister's voice rose as she asked that question.

"No! No, I haven't— No, she's not ready for that."

"So you're pretending to be engaged?"

"I'm pretending to be engaged, but I want to really be. Only every time I try to tell her this engagement is for real, she ignores me. I don't know what to do."

"Have you kissed her?"

"Well, yeah, you've seen me kiss her."

"That was for show. Have you in private?"

"I didn't think that would be a good thing to do. I might lose my head and—and I don't want to scare her."

Jessica rolled her eyes. "Surely you can kiss her without taking her to bed. I would think that's how you're going to convince her."

"But wouldn't she refuse me? I mean, I need to gain her trust, not destroy it."

"Pete, I shouldn't tell you this, but Mary Jo loves you—so much. She can't tell you no. If you love her, then everything's perfect!"

"Sh-she loves me?" he asked, dazed.

"Yes, she's loved you all along. But you broke her heart when you slept with that other woman. And you'd better not break her heart again, because you won't get a third chance."

"I know. I just need to—to figure out how to convince her."

"Well, while you're thinking about that, I'm going upstairs to interrupt my husband's paperwork. Remember, don't break her heart again."

Pete sat there staring into space as he took in his sister's words. Mary Jo loved him. That was the most amazing thing he'd ever heard.

Mary Jo was relieved when Pete followed Jessica out of the kitchen. It was so hard to act natural around him. Sometimes she forgot that she wasn't supposed to love him. To her, he was awfully lovable!

But she was supposed to be standoffish with him, except when the others were around. When people surrounded them, it wasn't so hard. Alone with him, however, she was at a loss.

What had he meant when he said he loved her? Was he serious?

The phone rang and she answered. It was a woman asking for Pete. "Just a moment, please," Mary Jo said.

Putting the phone down, she stepped to the door of the kitchen and called his name.

"Yeah?" he said, coming out of the living room.

"Telephone for you, Pete."

"Who is it?"

"I don't know."

He answered the phone and Mary Jo turned away, not wanting to hear his conversation.

Slamming down the receiver a moment

later, he said, "Why didn't you tell her I wasn't here?"

"Tell who?" she asked.

"That woman! She wanted to invite me to a party."

"What did you say?"

"I said of course…as long as I brought my fiancée with me."

"What did she say to that?"

"She said she hadn't heard I was engaged."

"I see."

"That's a very calm reaction."

"Yes, it is."

Pete stepped closer to her. "Why doesn't that upset you?"

She shrugged her shoulders. "It's none of my business."

"Damn it, it is, too. I've committed to you. I love you!"

"Pete, maybe it's time to end this arrangement."

"No! No, I don't think so. We're going to be married!"

She drew back from him. "I have to go to my room."

"Mary Jo, wait. We need to talk."

But she hurried away and closed her door.

Pete reached for another cookie and munched it thoughtfully. He'd told her the truth; he believed they were going to marry. But she wouldn't accept that.

The advice Jessie had given him crossed his mind. He wasn't convincing Mary Jo with his words. Would she believe his kisses more?

"Hey, I won't mind trying that," he admitted out loud.

But could he keep control of himself while he was convincing her?

Being so close to her went to his head, his heart, his body! He hadn't intended to take her to bed before. In fact, seducing the guest had been partly due to his time with Mary Jo. Making love to her had scared him to death. He'd tried to prove that she didn't matter, while knowing, deep down, that she did. Only he hadn't been mature enough to face that fact.

He'd grown a lot after breaking his leg and listening to Jim, who'd told him he'd made a mistake and would have to pay for it.

"And I've been paying every day since then," Pete muttered ruefully.

MARY JO STAYED in her room until it was time to start cooking.

Jessica and Leslie arrived in the kitchen just after she did. Mary Jo gave them jobs that needed to be done and the three of them worked together.

When Pete entered the room, Mary Jo knew it at once. Not because she saw him, but because she sensed his presence.

His arms went around her and he kissed her neck. "Hi, sweetheart. Is there anything I can do to help?"

"You could set the table in the dining room, if you want."

"Sure. How many will there be?"

"Everyone but Hank. He said he was going into town as soon as he got in," Mary Jo said.

"He can't even eat with his family? What's wrong with him?" Pete asked.

Mary Jo didn't answer, but Jessica didn't

hesitate. "Don't you remember? You once thought the same way."

"Yeah, but not anymore. I'm hanging out with the only lady I want," he said with a grin.

Leslie laughed. "I like that, Pete!"

He returned her smile as he counted out the silverware. "Okay, I'm off to set the table."

"It's so nice to see Pete helping out," she said when he'd left.

"It is," Mary Jo agreed.

"Has he really been helping you?" Jessica asked.

"From the first night, he's insisted on helping clean up after dinner. And when Hank came up with the new schedule, Pete told him they would cook their own breakfast and clean up after themselves. It's made my job much easier."

"Yes, Cliff mentioned what a turnaround Pete has made," Leslie said.

Jessica nodded. "Well, I'm certainly impressed."

Pete came back into the kitchen. "Okay, the table's set. What else can I do?" He looked around. "Has the iced tea been made?"

"No, not yet," Mary Jo said.

"I'll make it."

"You know how to do that?" Jessica looked amazed.

"Sure. Mary Jo showed me once."

"And I was impressed with you setting the table. That's wonderful, Pete."

"Thanks, Jess. Mary Jo recognized my potential!"

His sister laughed. "Oh, really? Does your potential have anything to do with Mary Jo's appearance?"

"It has everything to do with her appearance. And with her sweetness. And just with her. Everything in the world."

"Pete!" Mary Jo exclaimed. "You shouldn't say that!"

"But it's the truth, sweetheart. What can I say?"

Chapter Twelve

During dinner that evening Mary Jo thought she could relax with Jessica and Leslie, because finally Pete was kept busy talking with Cliff and Jim.

But she was wrong.

Three times he put his arm around the back of her chair, touching her spine and playing with her hair. Once he even leaned over and kissed her cheek.

The man was driving her crazy!

She debated what to do. She could simply tell him she couldn't wear his ring anymore. But hadn't she tried that? It hadn't worked.

She could leave the ranch. But the Lazy L had become home. The last thing she wanted to do was go back to her parents' café.

But she had to do something. And a happy ending didn't look possible.

"Hey, Mary Jo, Jim and I are going to watch a movie tonight. Do you want to join us?" Jessica asked.

"Oh, I—I don't know."

"Sure, we'll watch it with you," Pete said. "At least, we will if Mary Jo pops some popcorn."

"But you just had cheesecake! How could you want anything else to eat?" Jessica asked.

"We need popcorn to properly evaluate the movie. Right, Jim?"

"Uh, I guess so."

"Will you make popcorn, Mary Jo?"

"Yes, of course, after the dishes are done."

"I'll help," Pete said.

"Well, I can't let you slave away while I sit with my feet up. I'll help, too," Jim said, grinning.

"Good. I don't guess Leslie and I have to help, then. We'll go home and put *our* feet up," Cliff said.

Leslie protested. "I want to see the

movie, Cliff. And of course you and I are going to help with the cleanup."

He grumbled, but they all knew he wouldn't go against Leslie's decision.

With so many helping hands, it only took about ten minutes to wash up and put everything away.

Then Pete looked at Mary Jo. "The popcorn?"

"Yes, Pete, I'll make popcorn and bring it in." She didn't mention that she didn't intend to sit by him. That would be her little surprise.

Jessica helped with the task. Then each of them took a large bowl and went into the living room.

Mary Jo's plan to sit far away from Pete didn't work out. There were only two places left, and she couldn't take the one by Jim. That left the one beside Pete. She sighed as she sat down.

Pete leaned over and asked, "Are you tired?"

"No, I—I'm fine."

"Well, here goes." Jim started the DVD after he dimmed the lights. He pulled Jessica against him and wrapped his arms around her. "This is the best way to watch a movie."

"Definitely." Pete grinned as he put his arm around Mary Jo. When he felt her stiffen, he said, "Just relax and enjoy the movie."

Mary Jo fought against his advice, but as the film began she finally relaxed against him. After all, no one could see them in the dark.

PETE THOUGHT it was a good movie. Then again, any film that allowed him to hold Mary Jo for two hours had to be good.

As soon as the credits ran, she jumped up, as if she wanted to get away as soon as possible. Pete stood also, taking her hand in his. "Did you like the movie, honey?"

"Not really. I don't think it's appropriate for kids."

"Is that what you thought, Jessie?" he asked.

"Yes, Mary Jo's right. The plot was a little hard to follow. Maybe we could show it after a kids' movie, and leave time in between for parents to put their children to bed." Jessica turned to her husband. "What do you think, Jim?"

"I agree. I think you should keep it just in case. We might even have times where there are no kids among our guests. You never know."

"How are the reservations going?" Pete asked.

"We've got a few for the first two weeks of December. Christmas week is filled, and the week after."

"Do you think we'll fill up?"

"I'm not sure. We might pick up a few guests in January. February maybe. We'll have the best snow then, from what I can guess." Jim looked at Pete. "Is that true?"

"Yeah, there's usually good snow for skiing around that time, but it's also really cold for outdoor activities. I don't know. I wouldn't have thought we'd get that much business in the winter season, but I'm trying to be positive. I'm willing to do whatever is needed."

Jim smiled. "I think you helped by getting engaged to the best chef in the valley!"

"Yeah, she is that, but that's not the reason I gave her a ring. She's also the sweetest chef in the valley." He pulled Mary Jo close.

"Pete!" she whispered in protest.

"Don't be modest, sweetheart."

She twisted out of his hold and started gathering the popcorn bowls and soda cans.

Pete immediately began helping her.

Jessica got up, too. "You certainly have improved Pete, Mary Jo. He never used to help with the dishes."

"He's being very thoughtful," she replied, not looking at him.

"The puppies will be wanting their milk soon, won't they?" Pete asked her.

"Yes. I'll go and warm it up."

No one moved as Mary Jo left the room.

Then Cliff asked, "Is everything all right?"

"Yeah, sure, Granddad," Pete said, but he didn't look at anyone.

"Is what I said working?" Jessica asked.

"I'm not certain. I guess time will tell."

"What's she talking about?" Cliff demanded, though Leslie tried to keep him quiet.

"I asked Jessie a question and she suggested something she thought I should do. I want to keep Mary Jo happy."

"Yes, that's important. We want to keep her here on the ranch. She's the best chef in the state," his grandfather stated.

"We want to keep her because she's a wonderful person," Pete corrected.

"Of course," Cliff agreed.

Pete turned and headed to the kitchen. "Did you put the milk on for our babies?" he asked Mary Jo.

"Of course. I think they're awake already, but they're not crying yet."

He went over to the box and lifted the puppies into his arms. "Yeah, they're awake."

"Here's a syringe. I'll take Goldie."

"Oh, really," he said with a grin. "I thought you'd ask for Cocoa."

His teasing brought a smile to her lips, which pleased him. She settled with Goldie in her arms and fed him his milk.

Pete said softly, "I'm going to miss times like this when they grow up."

"Me, too."

"Do you think having a baby will be even more fun?"

"I—I don't know."

"It's something to talk about, isn't it? In my opinion having a baby would be fantastic. A little person to take care of."

"I think it will be more work."

"Oh, really?" He winked at her. "I promise to help all I can. It would be convenient if you have the baby during one of our vacation times. Then Jessie can take over the kitchen."

"I think it's a little too… I mean, we're not… I don't want to talk about that."

"You're right. We've still got to plan a wedding!"

"No!" She shifted Goldie, upsetting him. He complained with a short yip.

"I've never heard him bark before," Pete said.

"I shouldn't have moved him. He was almost asleep."

"It's all right, sweetheart. I shouldn't have upset you."

She didn't speak to him, a sure sign that she was upset.

Pete kept his eye on her. When Cocoa had finished all the milk, he took him to the box and put him down. Then he rinsed out the syringe he'd used.

When Goldie finished his milk, Mary Jo put him in with Cocoa. The two puppies snuggled together. She went to the sink to rinse her syringe in turn. Pete stood by the cabinet, not wanting to get too far from her.

As she moved away from the sink, he reached out and wrapped his arms around her. "Where are you running off to?"

"I—I thought I'd go to bed."

"Don't I get a good-night kiss?"

"No. There's no one to see, Pete. We don't have to pretend."

"Who's pretending?" he asked, before he dipped his head and kissed her.

His lips clung to hers, searching, conveying his feelings, until his tongue took over the task. As he deepened the kiss he pulled her tight against him. He couldn't get enough of her closeness.

She wrapped her arms around his neck, returning his kiss…and then, abruptly, withdrew.

"Where are you going, sweetheart?" he asked her.

"To bed…alone." She slipped into her room and shut the door.

Pete stood there, staring at the closed door that had once been open to him. But he wouldn't give up. He couldn't.

Tomorrow was another day.

ANOTHER STORM CAME IN that night. When Mary Jo got up in the morning, the windows were coated with white. She couldn't see if the snow that had fallen was still blowing about or if more was coming down.

She began mixing up pancake batter, and made sure the coffee was on, ready for anyone who woke up. Jim and Pete came in together, and she immediately filled a mug for each.

"Thanks, sweetheart," Pete said. "Did Hank go out at the regular time?"

"I don't know," Mary Jo said as she put Jim's coffee in front of him. "Is Jessica up?"

"No, not yet. We...we were up late last night." Jim kept his gaze fixed on his cup.

Pete looked at Mary Jo, wishing he could say the same thing.

He noticed her bright red cheeks, showing she understood what Jim was saying.

"Pancakes?" she asked. When the two men nodded, she began cooking.

They had finished breakfast and were enjoying a second cup of coffee when Jessica appeared. "I'm sorry I'm late," she said sleepily.

"No problem. Do you want pancakes?" Mary Jo asked.

"Oh, that sounds so good." She moved to the coffeemaker, poured herself a cup and sat down by her husband. "How long has it been snowing?" she asked as she took a sip of coffee.

"When we got up to feed the puppies, it had just started," Pete explained. "Hank went down to the barn, but I don't know if he actually rode out or if he's waiting for the snow to stop. It's coming down hard."

Jim frowned. "Maybe we should go to the barn to see what's going on."

"Yeah, you're probably right. But I'd rather stay here with Mary Jo."

He had his gaze fixed on his fiancée. Her cheeks reddened, but that was the only sign that she'd heard what he said. He finished his coffee and stood. "Okay, Jim, let's go."

Stepping to Mary Jo's side, Pete dipped his head to kiss her, but she turned away. Rather than plead for her attention, he walked out of the kitchen.

Jessica kept her gaze on Mary Jo and saw the sadness in her eyes as she watched Pete depart. Then Jim swept her into his arms and gave her a kiss that would keep her warm all day.

After he left the kitchen, Jessica asked, "Why didn't you give Pete a goodbye kiss?"

"I—I couldn't… I don't know."

"It can be dangerous going out in a storm like this."

Mary Jo began cleaning up from breakfast, trying to downplay her worry for Pete.

After the kitchen was tidy, Jessica suggested Mary Jo show her the bingo prizes. But even as she explained the story behind each, Mary Jo looked distracted. Jessica knew she was worried, especially since the storm seemed to be getting worse.

"I bet the guys are all sitting down in the barn, telling stories. Cowboys are good at that," Jessica said, trying to allay her friend's fears.

"Aren't you worried?" Mary Jo asked.

"Yes, a little." She put her arm around her. "Look, why don't I go check on them while you figure out what to fix for lunch?"

"Would you?"

"Sure."

"Don't get lost, Jessica."

"It's all right. I'm certain Hank would have strung ropes as a guide."

Mary Jo watched as Jessica put on her weather gear and left. Then she took a deep breath. What if she'd refused Pete a kiss and he got lost in the storm? She would never forgive herself.

"God wouldn't be so cruel," she muttered. To dispel those grim thoughts, she immediately began making a pot of soup and slicing cheddar for grilled cheese sandwiches. They were comfort foods, and right now she needed comfort.

Nothing was wrong, she told herself. Pete was going to be fine.

Firmly fixing her mind on a happy ending, she worked on a cobbler. Pete's favorite dessert. Not that his feelings about cobbler had anything to do with her decision, of course.

Oh, who was she kidding? She made it for Pete.

And hoped profoundly that he'd make it back to eat it.

PETE AND JIM ARRIVED AT the barn, feeling they'd walked miles. Inside, they found Hank and several cowboys sitting around a heater.

"Hey, aren't you riding out today?" Pete asked.

"Naw," Hank said, "it's too bad out there. We're waiting for the storm to end. Then we'll go see how the cows survived, give them some hay, make sure the ice is chopped up in the water tank."

"Need us to hang around and help?" Jim asked.

"Nope. If I need more hands, I can draft some of the guys who aren't working. We'll be fine."

"Well, since we're here, we might as well thaw out before heading back in that storm," Jim said.

"Sure. We can give you some space." Hank motioned for the cowboys to scoot over and give them access to the warmth.

Jim settled on an empty chair, while Pete decided to stand near the heater. "We can't stay too long. Mary Jo worries when I—when anyone goes out in a snowstorm."

"I thought she was raised in Colorado," one of the cowboys said.

"Wyoming, actually. Not far from here, though," Pete said.

"Have you heard any forecasts?" Hank asked.

Jim answered that question. "Yeah. The radio said it was predicted to end by nightfall."

"So we're wasting our time?"

"Pretty much, except for chopping holes in the water. The cows will need to drink."

"So you're telling me I can't go into town tonight?" Hank demanded.

"Yeah, pretty much," Pete said firmly.

"I don't think that's fair," his brother protested.

"Why not? I work tomorrow morning."

"Actually, Pete, I'm going to work tomorrow and Thursday." Jim looked at Hank. "I could work tonight, if you want to go to town."

Pete frowned at Jim. "I don't think you should make that offer. Hank needs to work tonight."

"You wouldn't say that if you were the one who was supposed to work late," Hank retorted.

Pete wanted to argue, but Jim shook his head. "It's fine for you to go to town, but I don't think you should drive until the snow has lessened. It would be too dangerous."

"No one should venture out in one of these blizzards, not until the snow and winds die down," one of the cowboys said.

"Yeah, but I don't want to waste my time sitting here."

"Then come back to the house and stay warm until it's clear enough to drive to town," Pete suggested.

"I guess I will. Guys, go on back to the bunkhouse. One of us will call when we need you. Jim says he'll go out with you."

The cowboys left in a mass exodus. Soon only Pete, Jim and Hank were left in the barn.

"I think we should leave the stove burning. It keeps the place warmer for the animals," Hank said, watching his brother as if he expected him to object.

"I agree, but I think we should move it to the center of the barn, and make sure there's nothing flammable close to it," Pete answered.

"I think that's—" Jim stopped so abruptly that Pete and Hank looked at him curiously. "Did you hear that?" he added.

Before either of them could ask what, the barn door was thrown back and a snow-covered form entered.

Chapter Thirteen

The newcomer was unrecognizable…until she pulled off her knitted cap. Jim jumped to his feet. "Jess? Is that you?"

"Yes, and I'm frozen!"

"Come over to the heater and warm up for a minute," Hank invited.

"A minute? It'll take lots longer than that! It's *cold* out there!" his sister exclaimed.

"What are you doing here, anyway? Is there an emergency at the house?" Pete asked.

"No. Just p-people are worrying."

"Mary Jo, you mean?"

His sister nodded. "She's real concerned about you."

"I'm heading back at once." Pete shrugged into his snow jacket and zipped it up.

"We'll follow you as soon as Jess is warmed up," Jim said, wrapping his arms around his wife.

"All right. Hank, you coming in?"

He shook his head, stating that he'd be heading straight to town.

Pete frowned in disgust, but said nothing to his brother. Opening the door, he stepped into the snowstorm, holding the guide rope tightly in his hand.

MARY JO WAS GROWING more and more impatient. Cooking relieved her anxiety a little, but not entirely. It was already eleven-thirty.

When she heard the back door open, she ran to see who had come in. She couldn't tell who it was for a minute, but then recognized Pete. In spite of her resolve to hold back, she rushed into his arms and kissed him.

Pete didn't hesitate; he wrapped his arms around her. With the heat they generated, he figured the snow would melt off of him in no time. His lips soon lost their numbness as he kissed her.

When Mary Jo pulled back, she whispered, "I was worried about you."

"I was careful, sweetheart."

"But it's like you're blind out there!"

"Which makes it doubly warm and cozy in here." He sniffed appreciatively. "I can smell a lot of good things. What are we having for lunch?"

"Homemade tomato soup, grilled cheese sandwiches and apple cobbler."

"You are great, sweetheart!" Pete leaned down at once to give her another kiss. "I bet Hank will wish he'd stayed for lunch!"

"He's out in the storm?"

"Not yet, but he's heading to town any minute now."

"But he can't see to drive in this! How will he stay on the road?"

"He's determined to go."

"But you can't let him! He could get stranded out there and die!" she protested.

"I don't think there's much I can do to stop him, honey."

Without another word, she headed for the phone. By the time Pete realized what she was up to, it was too late to intervene.

"Cliff, Hank is planning on leaving for town in this blizzard. I don't think that's a good idea," she was saying.

"Honey, Hank won't like you calling Granddad," Pete warned.

She ignored him. "You will… I'll make lunch for you and Leslie, too."

Pete took the phone out of her hand. "Granddad, coming for lunch is fine, but Hank is pretty determined." After a pause, he said, "Okay, Granddad." Then he hung up.

"Cliff and Leslie are coming," he told Mary Jo. "He's going to connect the rope and walk over."

"But how can he do that? He can't see, either! Oh, dear, I assumed they had already put up a guide line!"

Pete hugged her. "Sweetheart, he can do it. He'll take the end of the rope and walk until he runs into the big house. He'll be fine."

"I hope you're right. It'll be my fault if he gets lost in the storm." Tears were filling her eyes.

"He'll make it, no problem," Pete assured her, leaning down and kissing her.

Mary Jo couldn't hold back, worry making her reach out for contact. It might have led to a dangerous situation, but Jim and Jessica's arrival separated them before the kiss went any further.

"Oh! I'm—I'm glad you're back," Mary Jo stammered.

"Is everything okay?" Jim asked, looking at Pete.

"Yeah, we're fine. Where's Hank?"

"He's coming right behind us, but still says he's going into town."

"I called Cliff and told him," Mary Jo confessed. "He's coming over, along with Leslie."

"I'm not sure that's a good thing," Jim murmured. "Hank seems intent on getting to town at once."

"But he could go off the road in the blizzard. He—"

Jessica stepped closer to her friend. "He's used to driving in snow, Mary Jo."

"That doesn't make it safe!"

Cliff came in the back door just then.

"Where's Leslie?" Mary Jo asked.

"She'll be here in a minute. She had to wait until I connected the rope."

"How will she know?"

"I shook the rope, and she was holding the other end." He turned back to the door. "Here she is," he exclaimed, reaching out for her.

"I'd better start making sandwiches," Mary Jo said, retreating into the kitchen.

"I'll come help you as soon as I warm up," Jessica offered.

The door opened again and Hank rushed in, escorted by a cloud of snowflakes.

Cliff looked at him and said sternly, "You aren't going to town until the blizzard dies down. It's stupid to drive in this storm!"

"I can make it!"

"No, and you won't try!"

"You're not my father!" Hank yelled.

"No, I'm not, but I'm the closest thing to a father you have. You'll sit down and eat lunch with us. Maybe the snow will let up later. But you can't start out for the Springs until it does."

Hank threw his scarf across the floor and stomped into the kitchen. Though he saw Mary Jo, he ignored her and carried on to his room.

Cliff followed, keeping on Hank's heels at a pace that belied his years.

"Do you think we should follow them?" Jim asked.

Pete shook his head. "Nope. When they get like this, it's best to let them talk it through on their own." He motioned to the dining room table. "Let's go sit down and get out of their way."

MARY JO COULD FEEL the tension at the table. Unlike a normal lunch, hardly anyone spoke, least of all Hank.

She got up to start preparing the dessert, and as soon as they'd finished the sandwiches and soup, brought out the cobbler and coffee.

Pete grinned at her. "Good lunch, sweetheart."

"Thank you, Pete." She ducked her head and took a bite of her dessert.

"He's right, Mary Jo. This was a great lunch," Cliff declared.

She smiled at him, but wasn't sure if Cliff had actually tasted the food he ate, there was so much tension in the room. He might be chiming in just to act as if everything was normal.

Hank got up to refill his coffee cup. When he came back to the table, instead of sitting down, he announced that the storm seemed to be lessening.

Cliff immediately got up to go look out the window himself, with Hank on his heels.

"Aren't you going to check, too?" Mary Jo asked Pete.

"Nope. Granddad will decide."

"But what if Hank doesn't listen to him?"

"Honey, Granddad knows what he's doing."

"But—" Mary Jo began.

Pete leaned over and kissed her, effectively silencing her.

Cliff came back into the dining room just then, and they all heard the back door swing shut.

"He's right. The snow is letting up now,"

the older man announced. "I don't know for how long, though. I hope he makes it."

No one said anything.

Feeling uncomfortable, Mary Jo stood and began clearing the table. Jessica and Leslie helped, too.

When they finished cleaning the kitchen, Mary Jo said, "Leslie, you and Cliff are welcome to stay the day with us, if you like."

"I think we won't. I fear Cliff's argument with Hank took a lot out of him. But thanks for inviting us to lunch. It was wonderful."

"You're welcome."

After Cliff and Leslie went home, Mary Jo told Jessica she was going to go rest until the puppies needed to be fed.

"Jim and I can feed them at two, if you want us to," her friend offered.

She didn't hesitate. "That'd be great. Be sure and use canned milk for them."

"Yes, I know. We'll be careful."

"And you might tell Pete. That way he won't worry."

PETE WAS STILL SITTING at the table with Jim when Jessica entered the dining room. He turned around, looking for Mary Jo, then frowned and asked the question Jessica expected.

"Mary Jo wanted to go rest for a while. I promised her Jim and I would feed the puppies."

"And she agreed to that?" Pete asked.

"Yes. She seemed a little tired."

"Yeah, but I can't believe she's letting you feed Goldie." After a minute he said, "I think I'll go talk to her."

"But what if she's already asleep?"

Jim put a hand on his arm. "Maybe Jess is right, Pete. I think she was worried about Hank and Cliff having a fight."

"I know she was. She felt bad about calling Granddad."

"Was that what happened?" Jim asked.

"Yeah. I should've been the one to call him, but she never hesitated."

"Maybe she just needs some time to herself," he suggested.

Pete frowned. "You think she doesn't want to see me?"

"I don't know. Maybe she just needs some rest."

"Okay, but I'll help feed the puppies."

"That's a deal," Jessica said, smiling.

WHEN THE PUPPIES AWOKE, the three rushed into the kitchen. Jessica put on the milk to warm, and Jim and Pete held the little animals.

"They really are cute, aren't they?" Jim asked.

"Mary Jo and I think so. She favors Goldie, but Cocoa is mine."

"Well, I like both of them," Jessica said.

"Me, too." Jim petted Goldie, and the puppy licked his hand.

Jessica handed Pete one syringe, then reached for Goldie. "I get to feed Mary Jo's puppy."

"But I want to feed him," Jim protested.

She leaned down and whispered in his ear. He stood and let her sit down in his chair, then handed the little dog to her.

"Did my sister threaten you?" Pete asked with a grin.

"Yeah. I think she's tougher than me," he stated.

"No surprise." Pete's gaze traveled to the

door through which Mary Jo had disappeared.

"She'll be up by four, Pete. She's making stew for dinner. It'll just be the four of us," Jessica told him.

"That will be nice," he said.

"Yeah, it will." Jim grinned at him. "When you and Mary Jo are married, it will really be nice."

"*If* we get married."

"What are you talking about?" his brother-in-law asked.

"Didn't Jessie tell you?" Pete was surprised.

"I didn't know if I should," Jessica hurriedly said.

"Tell me what?"

"Mary Jo thinks we're pretending."

"What?" he demanded, consternation on his face.

"Jim, Pete loves her!" Jessica insisted.

"That doesn't explain why you didn't tell me!"

"Pete spoke to me in confidence. We discussed his progress. I didn't see any need to inform you," she replied stiffly.

"Jim, I assumed… I didn't ask her not to tell you."

When his sister glared at him, Pete realized he'd said the wrong thing.

"I mean…I love Mary Jo. I've been true to her ever since I broke my leg."

"That's good, Pete, but I think you should be honest with her."

"I have been! That's why I talked to Jessie about it. I didn't know what to do. She doesn't believe me," Pete finished, sounding more discouraged than ever.

"I'm sorry, Pete. I didn't realize—Maybe we should discuss what's going on with Mary Jo."

"I don't know what's going on with her. I've tried to tell her we're going to get married. I've talked to her about having children together. She backed away even farther." He shook his head, thoroughly frustrated. "I don't know what to do."

Chapter Fourteen

Mary Jo was adding onions and carrots to her stew when she heard a sound behind her. Whirling around, she found Pete a few feet away.

"You're up," he said, his voice husky.

"Yes. Did the puppies do all right for their feeding?"

"Yeah, but I think Goldie missed you."

She smiled. "I doubt that."

"Then how about I missed you."

"Don't be silly," she said dismissively.

"I'm not. I miss you whenever you aren't with me."

"Will Jim and Jessica be ready to eat around six?" she asked, hoping to distract him from his ridiculous remarks.

"I suppose."

"Did Hank call to let us know he got to town safely?"

"Why are you so worried about him?"

She blinked several times, not knowing how he could ask that. Finally, she said, "Because he's your brother."

After a moment, Pete said, "Yeah, he called. He got there all right."

"Good."

She returned her attention to her cooking, and Pete took the opportunity to move closer to her. Sliding his arms around her waist, he pressed his lips against her neck.

Mary Jo shrieked at the unexpected touch.

"Sweetheart, it's just me, not the bogeyman!"

"You snuck up on me. You should cough or something."

He covered his mouth for a fake cough. "Is that better?"

She nodded, but her eyes were wide, watching him.

This time he faced her as he reached out for her, sliding his arms around her waist and lowering his mouth to hers. A long minute later, he whispered, "I love you, Mary Jo."

She jerked her head away. "I have to fix dinner."

"I thought we were having stew?"

"Yes, but I need to do other things." She pulled herself out of his hold.

"Like what?"

"That's none of your business!"

"I think it is. I think you're using your work as a way to avoid me!"

"Am I required to account for my time to you? I don't think that's in my job description!"

"Sweetheart, all I'm trying to do is convince you that I love you."

She put up her hand to stop him. "No one is listening, Pete. Not even me." Then she ran to her room and slammed the door.

MARY JO SAT IN HER ROOM reading a book. At least that was what she intended to do. But her thoughts kept flitting away from the page. Then she'd have to find her place and try again.

She knew she'd have to return to the

kitchen at five forty-five. The expectation of finding Pete there waiting for her made her want to skip dinner. She wasn't interested in a cozy dinner for four.

Maybe she could eat early? No, that would just draw more attention from Pete.

She needed to remain calm. She had come to a decision earlier and she simply had to stick with it.

She was leaving the Lazy L.

But her departure would have to wait until Friday, when Pete went to work. She'd slip out right after he left. She and Goldie. No, on second thought, she couldn't take the dog with her. It wouldn't be right to separate the puppies, especially after they'd already lost their siblings.

She'd just have to go alone.

Ever since Pete started to believe their engagement was real, she'd known leaving was inevitable. Oh, she wanted it to be real, but believed Pete was sacrificing himself to keep the dude ranch operational.

She wanted a marriage that was based on love, not on good cooking.

The Ledbetters would be able to hire another chef before the winter tourist season started. If Pete liked the new cook, he wouldn't complain. After all, that was what concerned him. Right?

He sure was a good actor. When he kissed her, he felt so sincere, so genuine. She'd had to back away several times for fear they'd end up in bed once more. She couldn't, wouldn't make that mistake again. She'd repeated to herself that he was in love with good food, not her. It had become her mantra.

Now it was time for another performance. She had to keep Pete at a distance. The best way was through his stomach.

She went to the kitchen and dished up the stew, then stood at the door and called, "Dinner!"

Pete and Jim came from the living room and Jessica from upstairs.

"I was going to help you, Mary Jo. Why didn't you call me sooner?" she asked.

"Your turn will come in November." Mary Jo smiled at her friend.

"I know. But I bet you help me, anyway!"

"We'll see." She didn't want to lie to her, but couldn't tell her about her plan to return to Wyoming.

She was going to miss Jessica when she left. They'd spent so many years together. And, needless to say, she would miss Pete most of all.

"Hey, you've already served us? The stew smells great," Pete said, pausing to hug her on the way to his seat.

Just as she was sitting down with the others, Mary Jo heard the small yips that Goldie gave when he wanted her attention. Slipping from her chair, she went back to the kitchen.

Both puppies were climbing out of the box. She scooped them up in her arms, holding them as they tried to lick her.

"You sillies. Want to explore a little before you get your milk? I've got a ball you can play with." She sat down on the floor and rolled the red ball toward the puppies. They tumbled over each other, trying to get to it.

She was laughing at their antics when Pete came through the door.

"Mary Jo? Where are you?"

"Down here with the puppies."

He came around the island and peered down at her. "Aren't you going to eat your dinner?"

"Eventually. But the puppies wanted to play a little before they got their milk."

"Can't they wait?" he asked.

"Not really."

"But, Mary Jo, you have to have dinner."

"I can reheat it later. Go back and eat."

"I'll wait for you."

"That will just make more work for me, Pete. Go on."

He shot her a frustrated look, not wanting to do as she asked, but she didn't leave him an option. Stalking back to the dining room, he sent her a glance over his shoulder that said he wouldn't be gone long.

When the door closed behind him, Mary Jo picked up Goldie and cuddled him. Then she picked up Cocoa, too. She wished she could take both puppies with her when she left, but she couldn't do that to Pete.

She tossed the ball again, watching the puppies try to chase it. She wasn't sure they could even see it too clearly. That's why she'd chosen a red ball.

She was rolling the ball yet again when Pete reentered the kitchen. "I said for you to go eat," she protested.

"I'm done. And I brought my dishes, to rinse them and put them in the dishwasher."

"How could you finish so quickly?"

"I wanted to come help you, so I took big bites."

"You'll make yourself sick."

"Nah. Cowboys learn to eat fast when they're on a roundup. If you don't eat quickly, you don't eat."

He sat down on the floor with her and caught Cocoa as the puppy ran by him. "Where are you going, little guy?"

"I think he was hoping to beat his brother to the ball."

"Oops, Cocoa, sorry about that." Pete grinned and set him down when Mary Jo rolled the ball again. "Go, boy, go."

They spent a few minutes playing together. Mary Jo couldn't resist the camaraderie she felt with Pete. As the puppies ran across the kitchen, chasing the ball, Jessica and Jim opened the door. The ball rolled through, the puppies in hot pursuit.

"Oh, no! Stop them!" Mary Jo called out.

Pete jumped up and ran after them, followed by Jim.

"I hope they catch them. They're so little, they might get lost." Mary Jo struggled to her feet.

Just then, the door swung open again, and each man entered with a puppy in his hands.

Pete raised Cocoa up in the air. "We found them. We just had to follow the bouncing ball."

"I'm glad. I'm putting on their milk now. Jessica, do you want to help Pete feed them?"

"Don't you want to feed Goldie?"

"No, I think I'll have my dinner, so I can get things tidied up later."

"Okay, I can help feed them."

Pete stared at Mary Jo, a question in his eyes. But she didn't respond. She went in and picked up her bowl, then heated it in the microwave as Pete and Jessica began feeding the puppies.

When it was hot, Mary Jo went into the dining room to eat. To her surprise, Jim came to keep her company.

"That was a good stew tonight, Mary Jo. I think the guests will like it, too."

"It's not a difficult dish to put together. Almost anyone could make it."

"Really?"

"Yes."

"You don't sound like you intend to be here."

She took a bite of the stew to give herself time to come up with a good answer. "I didn't mean that. It's just that our guests expect a more complicated dish for dinner. Something more sophisticated."

"Oh, I see."

"By the way, we've got leftover cobbler for dessert tonight."

"I'm very fond of your cobbler." He laughed. "But nothing pleases Pete more, I've learned."

"Dessert usually does make him happy," she said with a smile, as if she liked to please him. And she did. That was why she'd made the cobbler in the first place.

"Okay, I'll go rinse my dish and then put the cobbler in the microwave."

"Great. I'll go round up the other two."

When his pup was through eating, Pete came to the sink to wash his hands.

"I'd forgotten the cobbler," Mary Jo explained. "I'm glad I remembered it."

"Your cobbler is one of my favorites," Pete told her.

"Mine, too," Jim stated. "My sweet wife said we'd be having it for dessert, but she was distressed by the puppies and forgot to remind Mary Jo."

On the way to the table with his cobbler à la mode Pete leaned over and kissed Mary Jo. She pulled away at once. She should've known he would respond to cobbler.

Maybe she should bake something he didn't like. He'd vote for a new chef at once.

But she was too proud of her cooking to screw up like that. She wanted him to remember her culinary talent, if nothing else.

"'Pride goeth before a fall,'" she whispered to herself.

"What did you say, Mary Jo?" he asked.

"Nothing."

"Are you sure?"

"Yes, I'm sure."

She was completely sure she had summed up her problem. But she didn't want to announce it to the other three.

Chapter Fifteen

The next two days, Pete wasn't working, and Mary Jo began to think of him as her shadow. The only time she had to herself was when she went to her bedroom. But she didn't go to her room much because she was baking desserts and freezing them. That way Jessica would have less work when she was cooking.

Her friend, however, had begun to notice what she was doing. "Do you think I don't know how to bake?" she asked curiously.

"I know you can, but since I have so much time off, I thought I'd help out."

"But Pete is off, too. Don't you want to do something with him?"

"I don't think we want to go horseback riding in the snow. It's too cold for that. Maybe we'll watch another movie tonight."

It would be dark, and if she kissed Pete, the others wouldn't think anything of it. She loved kissing him, but she didn't want anyone to notice.

"Oh, that's a good idea. I hope Jim feels up to it."

"Yes, and we could invite Cliff and Leslie, too."

Jessica gave her a strange look. "Do you really want so many people around?"

"Yes, I do. I miss Leslie, and Cliff is nice to me." Besides, it would be her last time to see them. Today, she noticed, everyone and every activity was taking on special meaning.

"Okay, I'll call them in a little while."

"Thanks, Jess," Mary Jo said, using Jim's nickname for his wife. "You can invite them for dinner, too."

"Too bad we can't convince Hank to stay home for an evening."

"I don't think you should try for that. It will only irritate him and upset Cliff."

"True." After a moment, Jessica asked, "Where is Pete now?"

"I think he said he was going to the barn."

"What for?"

"I didn't ask him." In fact, she'd given thanks that he had something to do that didn't leave him looking over her shoulder.

"Maybe he had to check on something for Jim. Are you sure he won't mind watching a film tonight?"

"He's usually pretty agreeable."

"Yeah, he has been, hasn't he? I didn't think he'd come around as nicely as he has. He was ornery in the beginning, but I think Jim had a good effect on him. You did, too."

"I don't think I should get any credit, Jessica."

"Well, I do!"

"Thanks, but I think any chef would have had the same effect."

"I don't think my brother would've been kissing a male chef!" Jessica laughed.

Mary Jo joined her. "Maybe not."

Jessica immediately turned the conversation to the subject of dinner. It made Mary

Jo think of Pete. Maybe it was a Ledbetter family trait, thinking about food.

Because it was her last meal at the ranch, Mary Jo wanted to do her best for tonight, so she decided on lasagna, which she knew was one of the family favorites. And for dessert, she'd baked a cake earlier in the day.

It was five o'clock when she reentered the kitchen for the final preparations. She'd spent the afternoon thinking of how this would be her last evening with Pete. No matter how she'd warned herself not to, she'd fallen in love with him. In fact, she'd been in love with him since the summer. It had been torture to deny herself his touch all these months. Tonight she intended to indulge herself, to indulge every fantasy she'd conjured up starring Pete Ledbetter.

And then she'd go.

Pete came in a few minutes later. "Something smells good." He gave her a steamy look. "Something looks good, too."

She smiled at him. "It's lasagna. Do you remember when I made it a couple of weeks ago?"

"Of course I do. It was great!"

"It seems to be a dish your family likes. Cliff voted for it for dinner."

"Good for Granddad."

"But it takes a long time to make it, so you'll have to stay busy at something while I'm working."

"Okay. If you give me one kiss, I'll get lost."

She turned, put her arms around his neck and kissed him fully. For the first time, she let her lips take from his all she desired.

"Man, you're going to have to make lasagna more often if it puts you in this kind of mood!"

Mary Jo smiled at him. "That sounds good to me."

He snatched another kiss before walking out of the kitchen.

For a long time after he left, Mary Jo stood with her eyes closed, making a memory of Pete's kiss.

AFTER HIS SHOWER, Pete came into the kitchen, offering to help. He looked handsome, though dressed only in his standard jeans and fleece.

"Thanks, Pete, but I think almost everything is done." In fact, she'd taken extra care, putting a linen cloth and a centerpiece on the dining room table.

"You need to leave some things for us to do. You spoil us by being too efficient." He dropped a kiss on her lips.

"You deserve a good meal, don't you think?"

"Without a doubt. Otherwise, I'd steal you away now."

"And maybe I'd let you," she whispered.

He wrapped his arms around her. "Let's blow this joint and find someplace where we'll be alone."

"I can't do that, Pete. I'm the chef, remember?"

"Yeah, I know. But someday we'll get away."

"Someday."

"Is anyone here?" Leslie called out as she and Cliff came through the door.

"Go right on in. Dinner will be on the table in five minutes."

"Pete? Aren't you coming, too?" Cliff asked.

"In a minute, Granddad," he called, never taking his arms from Mary Jo.

"You'd better go sit down so I can serve. Otherwise Cliff will complain."

"I wish you'd agree to marry me. Then we could disappear for a while."

"I doubt it."

"I think we could. We'd have November free."

With a smile, she turned him around and gave him a gentle shove toward the dining room. "Go sit down."

He spun back and kissed her one more time before he did as she said.

Mary Jo took a deep breath after Pete went to the dining room. As good as it felt to kiss him, to touch him, it would feel twice as bad to walk away. But tonight she wouldn't let herself think about that. Tonight was for enjoying, for making memories.

EVERYONE LOVED HER lasagna.

"This is even better than it was the first time, honey," Pete said.

"Yeah, it's delicious," Jim declared. Cliff was too busy eating, until Leslie elbowed him.

"Hmm? Oh, Mary Jo, this is great!"

"Thank you."

After dinner, while the women were cleaning up, she told them she'd made an extra pan they could have for lunch tomorrow, if anyone would enjoy it.

Jessica jumped on the idea. "Of course we'd enjoy it."

"We would, too, if we're invited!" Leslie hinted.

"Of course you are. But I might take some time off and run home, if that's okay. You can heat it up, right, Jessica?"

"Sure, that's fine. How long will you be gone?"

"Just a couple of days. I haven't seen my parents for a while."

"I'm actually anxious to start cooking again. I'm not sure Jim believes I *can* cook," Jessica said with a smile.

"But I know you can. I have faith in you."

"Thanks, Mary Jo. I can't believe how well things have worked out. You've always been like a sister to me, and we get to work together. I never dreamed it would happen like it has."

Mary Jo reached out and hugged her. She was almost glad to be so choked up she couldn't talk, or she would reveal her plan. And she couldn't do that.

Gathering her emotions, she came up with a smile and backed away from Jessica. "We've been lucky, haven't we?" She cleared her throat. "Now, we really should go watch that movie or the rest of them may start without us."

As they settled around the TV, Mary Jo realized this evening wasn't going to be easy. She might have dodged a bullet with Jessica, but she still had the hardest part ahead of her.

Pete barely waited for the movie to start before he put his arm around her and pulled her close for a kiss. She gave herself over to it, feeling almost carried away. He was so persuasive she almost dropped her guard—and her decorum—and suggested they go somewhere alone. Good sense and good manners won out.

When the movie ended, she clutched Pete's hand. They both walked Cliff and Leslie to the back door as Jim and Jessica went upstairs. Then Pete pulled Mary Jo close for a good-night kiss.

She wrapped her arms around Pete and leaned her entire body in responding to him. Finally, she wasn't holding back.

"Baby, you're setting me on fire!" Pete whispered.

"Good," she replied. "Do you have any condoms?"

Pete went stock-still. "What?" he managed to say after a moment. "I mean why?"

She drew a shaky breath and let it out. "Because I want to sleep with you tonight."

He kissed her before he asked, "Are you sure? I don't mind waiting until our wedding."

Mary Jo could hardly believe her ears. Pete Ledbetter had said he'd wait? "Well, I don't want to wait."

He flashed that devilish smile of his. "In that case, I've got some condoms. And I'm ready to make love to you again. It's been so long." He kissed her deeply. "Your room or mine?"

"Yours, if you don't mind."

"Fine. But I'm so excited, I hope I don't rush it too much. I'll try to hold off as long as I can."

She kissed him gently, then nudged him toward his room. "Let's go. I don't want to undress out here in the hallway."

He opened his door and pulled her into his room. He didn't bother turning on the light before he kissed her again, reaching for her buttons.

She didn't hesitate to reach for his, too. After unfastening his shirt, she parted it and ran her hand over his strong chest.

Pete, too, was exploring. He had removed her bra and was stroking her warm flesh and kissing it. "Oh, sweetheart," he sighed, "I didn't think we'd ever be like this again."

"I know. It's been so long."

When she wrapped her arms around him and her breasts rubbed against his warm chest, Pete stilled her. "Honey, we've got to get undressed quickly. I'm not going to last long."

They both stepped back and stripped before she melted into his arms once more. His mouth clinging, his tongue already mating with hers, he picked her up and laid her on his bed. Then he pulled on the condom. When he joined Mary Jo on his bed, the sheer excitement of the moment carried her to the verge of sexual completion. Pete must have felt the same because he entered her without hesitation. As he rocked against her he looked into her eyes, and in the moonlight she could see the man she loved. It was what sent her over the edge, Pete coming along with her.

Afterward, he held her against him and they both settled down to sleep.

When Pete awakened her at four to make love again, she found it more satisfying, more exciting, more…loving. He almost convinced her that he loved her more than her cooking. But not quite.

They went back to sleep again, snuggled up together.

WHEN PETE HIT THE alarm button to turn it off, Mary Jo opened one eye. He leaned over and kissed her. "Go back to sleep, sweetheart. Sleep in. I didn't let you get much rest last night." He kissed her again, then rolled out of bed again to pull on his shirt.

Mary Jo couldn't turn away. She watched him dress. Then he came back and dropped another kiss on her lips. She couldn't keep from putting her arms around his neck and demanding a little more.

Finally he pulled away. "Sorry, baby, but I have to go to work. But you'll have my full attention tonight. Sleep well."

She actually did fall back asleep. When she woke up at eight-thirty, she dressed and went to her room. She got out some clean clothes and took a shower. She meant to be on the road before the others were up.

When she reached the kitchen, she realized Jim, Jessica and Hank were already at breakfast. “Oh, I’m sorry I overslept.”

“It’s not a problem, Mary Jo. I think you’re due a little break,” Jim said. “Jess said you were going to visit your parents for a couple of days.”

“Yes. Jessica said she’d handle the cooking. There’s another pan of lasagna, and I put a few things in the freezer.”

“I’m sure you’ve covered the whole amount of time you’ll be gone. We’ll be fine,” Jessica said.

Mary Jo swallowed her guilt. She would mail letters in town, so they’d know by tomorrow that she wasn’t coming back. She blinked her eyes rapidly, dispelling her tears. “Well, I’d best be on my way.”

“But wait. You haven’t had breakfast yet,” Jessica said. “Sit down and I’ll make some for you.”

Mary Jo couldn’t think of a good excuse to skip breakfast...except that she might not be able to keep it down.

After eating in a hurry, she again said she had to be on her way. Jim offered to carry her overnight bag out to her car, but she couldn't let him do that. If he saw all that was in there, he'd realize she wasn't coming back.

After saying a final goodbye to the puppies and making sure Jessica knew how to feed and care for them, Mary Jo hugged her friend and left. Getting into her car, she sighed in relief. Then she drove to the post office in Steamboat Springs. She sat in the vehicle, writing one more letter, to Pete. Keeping it brief, she told him where she'd left the ring he'd given her, so he could return it, or save it for the woman he truly loved.

Sealing the envelope, she gathered it and the other letters and took them into the post office. Smiling at the clerk, she handed them over. Then she got back in her car and headed out of town toward southwest Wyoming, tears streaming down her face.

JIM LOOKED AT JESSICA. "Did anything about Mary Jo seem strange to you?"

"No, not really. She's gone to visit her parents before. I don't think she's close to them, but maybe something's going on with them. Family problems."

"So she didn't explain why she was going home now?"

"No. But she's been busy, so I'm assuming she just wanted to go on a visit and rest."

Jim frowned as he stared into space. "I'm not sure she's coming back."

"Of course she is. She only took an overnight bag with her!"

"Are you sure?" he asked.

"I watched her get in her car."

"But maybe she took something out earlier?"

Jessica mentally reviewed what had happened that morning. "I'm going to look in her room. Just to check."

She left Jim sipping a second cup of coffee while she went to Mary Jo's room. She opened the door and got her answer.

There were no clothes in the closet.

Then she opened the chest of drawers and found it empty, too. The walls, which had been covered with awards Mary Jo had won over the years, were bare.

There was nothing in the room that indicated someone lived there.

Nothing at all.

Chapter Sixteen

Pete urged his horse to a lope to get back to the house. He'd missed Mary Jo today and wanted to hold her in his arms again. After making love to her twice last night, he looked forward to doing so once more, as soon as possible.

After tomorrow, he wouldn't have to work again for five days. And he intended to spend those five days in bed with his fiancée.

When he reached the barn, he unsaddled his horse and rubbed him down. Then he hurried to the house. As he came in the door, he called, "Mary Jo?"

There was no answer. He decided she must be upstairs with Jessie. He hurried past the dining room to the stairwell and called again. "Mary Jo?"

His sister came to the top of the steps. "Didn't Mary Jo tell you she was going home to her parents' place for a couple of days?"

Pete froze. "No. She didn't say anything to me about that."

"She probably forgot. I mean, she—she took her things with her."

"What?"

"I looked in her bedroom, Pete. She—she took everything!"

In a heartbeat he whirled around and ran to her room.

Several minutes later, Jessica and Jim appeared at the door. Pete was sitting on the edge of Mary Jo's bed, his face in his hands.

"Are you all right, Pete?" Jim asked.

"I can't believe… We made love last night. I thought we'd worked things out. And she left me!"

Jessica sat beside him. "You made love to Mary Jo last night? I thought you weren't going to do that until everything got resolved!"

"Everything *was* resolved! It was her

idea! We made love and then we made love again. I don't know what went wrong!"

"Maybe you should call her," Jessica suggested.

"I don't know. I'm afraid of what she'll tell me. If she said she'll be back in a couple of days, maybe I should wait until she arrives."

"Pete, did you find anything she didn't take? Anything she left behind?" Jim asked.

"No," he said, not looking up.

"So she took the ring, too?"

"I guess so. It's not here."

"Did she sleep in her bed last night?"

"No. When I left this morning, she was still in mine."

"Did she leave anything in there? Maybe a note for you?"

By the time Jim stopped talking, Pete had run to his room. Jim followed, and found him looking around his bed, on his chest of drawers, but he found nothing.

"Pete, I'm sorry. I didn't think she'd leave without a note or something."

He looked up at his brother-in-law. "That's just it, Jim. I don't believe she did."

PETE STARED AT the lasagna Mary Jo had made last night. "This doesn't make sense! She's left me, but she prepared food for all of us?"

"Mary Jo is a good friend, Pete," Jessica told him. "I don't think she would disappear and leave me holding the bag."

He shook his head. "No. I'm sure she'll be back."

"I'm not certain she will be," his sister said softly.

He shoved back his chair. "I'm not hungry!" he stated, and strode out of the kitchen.

As she watched her brother leave, Jessica felt her eyes fill with tears.

"Sweetheart, you can't let this get to you," Jim said as he put his arm around her.

"But she's my friend. And he's my brother."

"I know. Maybe she'll call tomorrow."

Jessica sighed. "I hope so. I don't want to

think about her not coming back." Her voice cracked as she added, "For Pete's sake."

AT 6:00 A.M., Jim came down to see if Pete wanted him to go to work for him. But Pete refused. Jim cooked him breakfast, telling Pete he had to eat before he went out.

Then Jim wandered back to his bedroom. He felt for Pete, but had no clue what Mary Jo was thinking. He looked at his wife, who was finally sleeping peacefully after crying all night. He slipped off his jeans and slid under the covers to sleep a little longer himself, gathering Jessica into his arms and holding her tight.

Later, when they got up and dressed, they went down to breakfast.

"While I make coffee, why don't you go get the mail, Jim. Maybe we'll have more reservations."

He went to the front door to gather the mail. There seemed to be an exceptionally large amount of it. He brought it back to the kitchen as he sorted it.

"Looks like we've got a lot of reservations."

"Oh, good. Mary Jo will—" Jessica gulped and then said, "Never mind."

Jim flipped past a couple more letters, then checked them again. "There are envelopes here addressed to you and Pete—Lazy L stationery."

She came to a complete halt. "Do you think they're from Mary Jo?"

"Maybe."

Jessica ran to her husband. "Where's mine?"

He handed it to her and sat down to wait for her to read it.

Jessica covered her mouth and a sob broke through. She wiped a tear from her cheek. "She says she's not coming back. She apologized for not being honest. She—she believes Pete was pretending to love her because he was trying to make the next season a good one. She said she couldn't pretend anymore. She couldn't be married to Pete unless he loved her. But she asked that I not tell him that."

"I think I'd better go get him."

"Do you know where he's working today?"

"I'll find him."

PETE HAD SHUT HIS MIND to thoughts of Mary Jo. The only way he could do his job was to focus on it. But when one of the cowboys pointed to a rider racing toward them, Pete knew at once that Jim knew something. He turned his horse and rode to meet him.

"She called?" he asked harshly.

"No. She sent this." Jim held out a letter.

Pete stared at the envelope.

"Don't you want to read it?"

As if awakening from a stupor, Pete reached out and took it. He looked at it from every angle before slowly opening the envelope. Then he took out the folded sheet of paper and slowly read the half-page note.

"What did she say?"

Jim's voice barely registered in Pete's hazy brain. "She told me where to find her ring."

"She didn't take it with her?"

"No. She wants me to save it for the woman I love."

"Why did she think you were kissing her and helping her with the work if you didn't love her?"

Pete finally looked at him. "She thinks I got engaged to her to keep her working at the ranch."

"You're kidding!"

"Not according to this letter." Pete shook his head as he folded the note and put it in his pocket.

"So what are you going to do?"

"I'm going after her. Can you cover for me?"

"Sure."

Pete rode toward the house without looking back.

PETE WANTED TO SEE Jessica first. Without preamble he asked, "What did she write to *you?*"

"I can't let you read it."

"Why not?" His voice was husky and stern, even to his own ears.

"Because she asked me not to."

"And you're gonna be her friend instead of my sister?"

Jessica looked down, for a long, silent moment. “Pete, Mary Jo has been my best friend for a long time.”

Though perturbed, he understood. “Okay, answer me this, then.”

“What?”

“Where do her parents live?”

“You’re going to go there?”

“Yeah, Jessie, I am. I have to convince her that I love her!”

“What did she write to you?”

“She said to save the ring for someone I love.” Repeating her words felt like a stab to his heart.

“And will you?” Jessica asked softly.

“Oh, yeah. I’m going to give it to her.”

“I think you’re doing the right thing, Pete.”

“So tell me where she’s from. Wyoming’s a big state.”

“She’s from a little town called Rock River.” Jessica gave him directions. She’d gone there once with Mary Jo while they were in college.

Not wasting another second, Pete strode

to the door. "I'll be back after I convince Mary Jo to marry me."

He was driving way too fast, Pete knew, but the roads weren't busy. He couldn't stand to wait any longer than he had to.

Three hours later, when he pulled into Rock River, it didn't take long to find the family restaurant Mary Jo's parents owned and operated. He parked in front, and figured there wouldn't be many people in the café at two o'clock. Walking in, he stopped to survey the scene.

Almost at once he spotted Mary Jo. The only person under fifty in the café, she was behind the counter, talking to a man as she poured him coffee.

Pete walked up and straddled a stool. "Any chance I can get some coffee, too?"

Mary Jo stared at him, not moving.

"What's wrong, Mary Jo?" the gentleman she'd been serving asked.

"N-nothing. I'll get a cup," she said quietly.

Pete waited until she'd poured him the coffee. It took all the patience he had not to jump over the counter, take her in his arms and carry her out of there, back to the Lazy L where she belonged. Instead, he casually asked, “Is the food good here?”

She stiffened again. “Yes, it’s very good.”

“You must be the cook.”

“What are you doing here, Pete?” Her cheeks were flushed.

“I’m doing what you told me to do.”

“What’s that?” she asked crisply.

“I’m giving my ring to the lady I love.”

She glared at him. “It’s time to end the game, Pete! You’ll have to find another chef!’

“I’m willing to do so. But that has nothing to do with the lady I love.”

She stood taller, her arms akimbo. “Fine! Go give her the ring! See if I care!”

“I hope you care. I *want* you to care.”

“What are you talking about?”

Pete reached into his shirt pocket and pulled out the ring he’d bought for her. “I think you forgot something.”

Her reaction was different from what

he'd hoped. Her eyes welled with tears and she ran to the kitchen.

The customer beside him cleared his throat. "Well now, son, you've gone and upset Mary Jo, which isn't very nice. We just got her back yesterday."

"I know you did, but she can't stay."

"Why not?"

"Because I'm going to marry her."

"Is that so?"

"Yeah. I think I need to go back there." He nodded toward the kitchen.

"I reckon you do."

Pete went around the counter and into the kitchen, calling, "Mary Jo, we need to talk."

But she wasn't alone. Another woman, older but the spitting image of her, stood beside her.

"I'm Mary Jo's mother. I don't think we've met."

He stuck out his hand. "I'm Pete Ledbetter."

"Yeah, I figured," she said as she shook it. "You're right, Mary Jo. He is good-lookin'. No wonder you can't trust him."

"But she *can* trust me. I'm in love with her."

"That's not what she says."

"I'd been telling her as often as I could. And she loves me."

"Did she tell you that?"

"Not in words, but she went to bed with me."

Mrs. Michaels's brows rose. "Oh, really? Did you use protection?"

"Of course." Then last night flashed back into his consciousness. They'd been so wrapped up in each other that they'd failed to use a condom. "At least the first time I did. I didn't remember to use one later."

Mary Jo's face was red when he turned to her.

"Did you realize that, sweetheart? That we didn't use any protection?"

"No, I didn't."

"I thought it didn't matter until I realized you'd left...and weren't coming back."

"I—I had to leave. I fixed as much food as I could and put it in the freezer."

"Mary Jo, Jessie can cook. We can hire

another chef. If you'll marry me, I'll support you. You don't have to be the chef if you don't want to."

"Why not?"

"Because you'd be my wife. You wouldn't have to work."

"But I am a chef."

"And a damn fine one, but I don't want you to think I'm proposing to you because of that. That's not what's important. Please take back your ring, Mary Jo."

"May I see it?" Mary Jo's mother asked.

"Yes, ma'am." He handed it to her. "I didn't get your name."

"It's Elaine. This is a mighty pretty ring. Has a lot of shine."

"Yeah. I wanted a ring Mary Jo would be proud of."

She handed it back to him. "This should do the job."

"But she keeps refusing it."

"Try her again," her mother said.

He went down on one knee. "Mary Jo, I love you and I'll be faithful to you forever, if you'll just believe me. Please?"

She took a step toward him. “Do you really mean it?”

“Yeah, honey. I’ve been meaning it ever since I broke my leg…and your heart. I want you back.”

“Oh, Pete!” Mary Jo cried, and flung herself into his arms.

“Well, I reckon we’re having a wedding.” Elaine Michaels folded her arms over her chest and surveyed the happy couple.

Pete raised his head. “Yes, ma’am. We’ll go get the license this afternoon.” He stood, helping Mary Jo to her feet. “And then I’ll go back home. But I’ll return on Sunday, and we’ll plan on having the wedding that afternoon or the next morning. Is that all right?”

“Mary Jo?” her mother asked. “Is that all right with you?”

“Yes, Mom.”

Pete kissed his fiancée again, something he could get very used to. “Let’s go get the license,” he urged, moving her toward the door.

“Her daddy will be here when you come back,” Elaine said as they left.

Outside, Pete said, "Was that supposed to scare me?"

"What?"

"Your daddy being back. Is he going to fight me?"

Mary Jo chuckled. "No, honey. Daddy won't scare you."

"Good. And I hope my family won't scare anyone, either, 'cause they're all coming here for the wedding."

"Jessica will be here?"

"Of course. She always said you were like sisters, and now you'll really *be* sisters."

Mary Jo's lips curved in a huge grin. "That's right! How exciting!"

"Hey, pay me some attention, too. I'm going to be your husband!"

"I know." Those same lips met his in a kiss he felt to his boots. "I'm a very lucky woman."

Pete kissed her again. "Not half as lucky as me."

* * * * *

Cowboy
at
Heart